BEDTIME READS

Janet Pywell

Bedtime Reads

ISBN: 978-1-9998537-0-9

Cover Art copyright @ 2017 Candescent Press

Published by Kingsdown Publishing

For more information visit: www.janetpywell.com

For Amanda

BEDTIME READS

Short Stories

Abyssinian Dropfoot
My Lost Brother
Letters Abroad
Aqua Tofana
A Pair Of Shoes
Something Might Happen
All Inclusive
All Exclusive
All Encompassing
Dating For A Dad
They Lied
Hattie
Jacob's Birthday
Just A Drag
I'd Lie In The Road For You
The Bar
Jan d'Artagnan

Abyssinian Dropfoot

'I'm not one to complain,' Harry said to his sister, Gloria.

'I know,' she replied, 'but Richard's only coming round for dinner and it won't be a late night – I promise.'

'It's just that this pain in my head doesn't seem to be shifting – I've had it for three days now.'

'I think some company will do you good – it will do us both good.'

'It's not just an ordinary headache, Gloria. It's been going on for too long.' He rubbed his temple, pinched his nose and sat at the kitchen table.

'I'm making cottage pie – your favourite,' she said opening the fridge and pulling out mince, carrots and onions.

'Is it serious?'

'I really like him Harry and I want you to get to know him. He's great fun and we share the same sense of humour.'

'Richard Collins,' Harry said, savouring the name. 'I don't remember him from school.'

'He remembers you and he's looking forward to seeing you again.'

'Was he sporty?'

'Yes – he goes to the gym now.'

'I didn't do any sport - don't you remember?'

'No,' Gloria said and began chopping and slicing. 'You can lay the table if you like?'

Harry stretched his neck and shoulders. The thought of having someone round for dinner wasn't his idea of a happy evening besides he wasn't really up to it. He didn't feel well.

'We'll eat in the dining room for a change. I'm sick of us eating at the kitchen table. We can light some candles. I bought some new ones today, in there.' She nodded at a carrier bag on the kitchen counter and Harry stood up and peered inside.

'You've gone to a lot of trouble – and expense…'

'I can afford it.'

Harry sat down again. He's never had Gloria's energy but since Gloria turned thirty she'd changed. She had even more vitality, more spirit.

'Is it your body clock thing again?' he asked.

'No – not this time – I think Richard is – the one.'

Harry leaned forward and put his head between his legs waiting for the blood to rush to his head. 'If I'm no better by tomorrow I'll have to go to the doctors again.'

'Of course you will,' Gloria replied but it wasn't the answer that Harry wanted. Of course he wouldn't be better by tomorrow, couldn't she see that? She had no idea how ill he was.

'Perhaps if you move around, it will get your circulation going,' she smiled. 'Richard will be here soon. Will you shower and change?'

Harry nodded. 'That's what I'll do. I'll go and get ready. My left arm has been hurting me all week and I find it hard to lift it above my shoulder. Look, I can't lift it very well and it's painful. It might take me a while to get ready so I'll go up now. You're not looking, Gloria. Look! I can only raise my arm to here. See?'

'Well, run hot water on your head and your shoulders and it might clear.'

'It's not as simple as that. I think it's something more serious,' he paused waiting for her to look at him but the potatoes were boiling and Gloria added a tin of oxtail soup to the frying minced beef. The kitchen was filled with warm aromas but Harry felt queasy.

'I'm not sure I'll be able to eat anything.'

'That's fine, Harry. If you want to eat later, you can – perhaps you'd like a lie down?'

'I want to meet Richard.'

'Ok.'

'Did you meet him at the gym?'

'He's in my art class.'

'On a Wednesday night? The one I couldn't go to because I had sprained my wrist?'

'Probably.'

'Don't you remember?'

'I can't think why you missed the first class.'

'I remember, Gloria. I tripped when we had that walk in the woods. You insisted on taking the short cut to the pub even though I said it was dangerous.'

'Right,' Gloria began mashing potatoes with butter and milk.

'You made me leek and potato soup afterwards.'

'Did I?'

'Yes. You said you would make my favourite thing in the whole world.'

Gloria laughed. 'Leek soup.'

'With potatoes.'

'Would you wipe some glasses for me and shine the cutlery while you are sitting there?'

Harry looked at the new tea towel she placed before him then she passed him knives and forks from the drawer. It saved him from standing up.

'Is he a good artist?' he asked.

'Brilliant – he makes Bansky look like an amateur. He's got his own web page. You should look him up?'

'I think that's what gives me the pain in my left eye and my headache. I think it's the Wifi – I may be allergic to it.'

'To the Wifi?'

'Yes – it can happen you know. It's the invisible rays that we can't see. That invisible power – it has a major effect on some people.' Harry polished and buffed the glasses as he spoke.

Gloria spooned the meat mixture into a dish, added mashed potato and then grated cheese on top. 'I'm going up to change,' she said.

'I'll sit here for a while. I feel a bit tired.'

'But you haven't done anything all day.'

'That's not true! I put the washing on this morning. All you had to do was to peg it on the line.'

Gloria sat opposite him at the table. She stared at him for a while and then she reached out and took his hand in hers.

'Harry, you're not ill.'

'You don't know that.'

'I do.'

'What about the tingling in my foot?'

'Harry, I really think that if you just got on with life and stopped thinking about your health every moment of the day then you wouldn't feel ill.'

'Do you think I am making it up?' Harry stood up pushing his chair away so it collided with the radiator on the wall.

'I'm concerned that you concentrate too much on your health. You went privately to see the doctor three months ago and he gave you a complete medical. You're fine. There's nothing wrong with you.'

'You have no sympathy, Gloria. You're a hard person. I hope that you're kinder to Richard − I really do. Now my head feels worse. You do this on purpose. That's the doorbell − is he early?'

'It seems like it.' Gloria rose from the table. She didn't check her appearance before answering the door and Harry listened as she greeted Richard in the hallway.

He heard them kiss - probably cheeks - and she whispered something he couldn't hear. Then they appeared in the kitchen together, arm in arm, looking happy and relaxed.

'Do you remember Harry?' she said, leaning against Richard's muscled shoulder.

'Of course, Harry − it's great to see you.' His handshake was strong and Harry winced. Richard was tall and rugged with a square chin covered in a fashionable trimmed beard. 'I think we were in the same year but not the same class.'

Harry frowned. 'I don't remember.'

'That's because you were the clever one with your nose

in a book in the library and I was the sports fanatic who wouldn't sit at my desk.' Richard beamed. 'Fat lot of good it did. Wasn't good enough to be a footballer and the only thing I could do was to work with my Dad.'

'Doing what?'

'I became an electrician.' Richard shrugged off his coat and hung it on the back of a kitchen chair. His eyes didn't leave Harry's face until Gloria bent down to put the cottage pie in the oven and then he studied her legs and shapely bottom.

'He still reads a lot.' When Gloria turned around she shared a smile with Richard.

'That's good, Harry. What do you read thrillers, crime, sci-fi?'

'Mostly medical journals.' Gloria replied for Harry.

'Do you study medicine?' Richard's eyes widen in surprise.

'No. I'm just interested in health. I work part-time in a care home.'

'Ah, a worthy job.' Richard took a Bud that Gloria offered him and drank from the bottle. 'Cheers. You not drinking?' he said to Harry.

'My stomach isn't right.'

'We'll eat in half an hour. I'll lay the table in the dining room,' Gloria said, lifting the cutlery and glasses.

'I've had these pains for a few days and I haven't been well for months,' Harry said wondering if Richard was listening. He didn't seem to be able to take his gaze from Gloria as she bustled in and out of the room, collecting salt and pepper, and matches for the candles.

'I exercise through pain,' Richard said.

'I couldn't do that. Besides it's not a muscular pain. It

would make me worse. I'd be seriously ill.'

'Seriously?'

Harry nodded.

Gloria came back into the kitchen and Harry noticed a softness in her eyes that wasn't there earlier.

'So, are you ill?' Richard asked.

'I haven't been feeling very well recently…'

'Have you got a headache?' Richard asked.

'Yes. How did you know?'

'One that hurts behind the eye?'

'Yes.'

'Do you feel tired?'

'Yes.'

'What about the rest of your body – any pains?'

'In my arm-'

'Oh goodness, I hope it's not…'

'What?' Harry leaned forward.

'That new virus, it's very serious. The one that they're trying to keep quiet - but a medical reporter has published an article and-'

'Where? What is it?'

'The symptoms are pains in the…right arm.'

'Mine is in my left,' Harry sighed and lifted his arm. 'See? It hurts.'

'Is that your writing arm?' Richard asked.

'No, the opposite.'

'That's what it said in the article. The pains are always in the opposite arm to your writing arm and you can only lift it to here or it hurts.'

Richard raised his arm to his shoulder height so their fingers almost touched.

Harry blinked. 'It hurts.'

'Do you get tummy pains?' Richard asked.

'Sometimes - yes.'

'All across here?' Richard's big hand touched his stomach.

'Yes.'

'And tell me, do you get short of breath.'

Harry's eyes widened. 'Sometimes…yes...'

Richard looked at Gloria and shook his head. 'This isn't good.'

Gloria turned away and Harry thought she had tears in her eyes.

'Tell me, what is it?' he asked.

'I can't be sure but it can't be a coincidence…'

'Do you think I have it?'

'You seem to have the same symptoms-'

'Is it serious?'

'It depends, if it's treated in time…'

'And what if they don't?'

Richard shook his head. 'Abyssinian drop-foot takes no prisoners.'

Gloria dropped the colander and it clattered in the sink.

Harry thought she was upset. Her shoulders were hunched over and they shook. He thought he would hug her and reassure her that he would be okay. Well, he hoped he would be. Since their parents died five years ago they lived together and she would be all alone if anything happened to him. He couldn't be ill. He couldn't possibly be sick.

'Is it life threatening?' he asked.

Richard stroked his beard. 'Well…it might be.'

'Why haven't I heard about it?'

'They're keeping a lid on it at the moment in case of an

epidemic.'

'Epidemic?'

Richard nodded. 'It comes from the Arctic.'

'The Arctic?' Harry thought for a second. 'Gloria, Mrs Melloway went on that cruise to the Arctic just a few weeks before she came into the home. She's only been back a month.'

'Oh, no!' Richard slapped his forehead.

'She did! Do you remember, Gloria? I told you. I said that since she came back, she wasn't herself. She had a sore throat and a temperature.'

'Have you got a sore throat?' Richard asked.

Harry felt the glands at the side of his neck. He stretched his throat muscles and opened his mouth wide as if yawning. He coughed and swallowed hard. 'It does feel a bit tight.'

'And what about your ears? Can you hear me alright?'

'I think so.' Harry shook his head and rocked his neck.

'Temperature?' asked Richard.

Harry leaned forward so Richard could feel for himself. His hand was cold on Harry's forehead.

'Oh, my goodness,' Richard said. 'You're extremely hot - too hot. I hope you haven't caught it.'

Harry swallowed. His throat felt swollen and sore and his voice rasped when he spoke. 'Abby what?'

'Abyssinian Drop-Foot.'

'Where is Abyssinia?' Harry looked at Gloria.

'Old Egypt,' she replied.

'So why does it come from the Arctic?' asked Harry looking at Richard.

'Dinner's ready,' Gloria called. She opened the oven and carried the cottage pie, using oven gloves, to the dining room.

'I think she's upset,' Harry whispered.

'It's a virulent virus that began in the middle-east but only became more rampant since it thrives on…cold weather.'

'And what happens?'

'It makes people's feet go numb. Have you-'

'Yes.' Harry rotates his ankle. 'I think I've got tingling in my-'

'It's best to stay hot and in isolation.'

'And if not?'

'You could be putting Gloria and me in danger.'

Harry's mouth dropped open and he covered it quickly with his hand. 'What shall we do?'

'I think what we should do is what the other people did – the ones who survived.'

'Survived? What did they do?'

'Twelve hours. Quarantine. Complete darkness.'

'Really?'

'Yes, because it seems that in the dark, our body generates bio-allergic atoms and combined with endorphins that our body produces when we are asleep, our body temperature rises and-'

'Sleep?'

'Oh, yes, you must sleep. There's a herb in a natural sleeping tablet – I can't remember the name of it now – but it's very special and when taken, you lay in the dark and sleep for ten hours and your body warmth increases, and all the symptoms disappear and you can be cured in a matter of hours.'

'I've got some herbal sleeping tablets.'

'No? Really –that's great news. Gloria,' Richard

shouted. 'Stay in the dining room just in case it's contagious and I'll take Harry upstairs and make sure he takes a herbal tablet. Come on, Harry. Let me help you.' Richard took Harry's arm and led him gently upstairs.

'That's kind. Are you sure you don't mind, Richard?'

'There's no need to worry. The other thing is music. Your body produces music-morphines that make you relax and allow the sleeping tablet to work more effectively. Oh, you've an iPod. Yes, definitely pop those in your ears, lie down and sleep and you'll be cured in no time.'

Downstairs Gloria smiled and took out her purse. She placed a crisp twenty on the table beside Richard's plate and sat waiting. She was happy she lost the bet. Everyone was happy.

Harry got the attention he wanted and they would have a candle-lit dinner after all.

She poured a glass of Burgundy and lifted it to the ceiling and the creaking boards upstairs: *to a romantic evening with Richard, the man of my dreams.*

But there was a tingling sensation creeping up her left-foot and the pain was spreading behind her eyes toward her temple.

My Lost Brother

He's arriving anytime soon. In fact, he's fifteen minutes late. I'm surprised. I emailed him my address. Perhaps he's lost? Could he have changed his mind? His messages sounded eager enough but he said he was busy. He's a carpenter - just like Jesus.

I'm talking aloud and staring out of the window into the tree lined street of my suburban home.

Will we look alike? Will he have my blonde hair and blue eyes like our mother? If only she was still alive to know that we are meeting today. Forty-five years after she gave him away.

She was a drug addict. I was two when I went into care. I was fostered and eventually when I was seven my parents adopted me. She had died by then and I had forgotten her.

Karl was taken from birth. I wonder if he remembers her holding him but how could he? Who remembers the first few weeks of their life? I don't remember her even being pregnant.

That's the doorbell.

That's Karl. 'Ohmygod! Ohmygod! I hope he likes me.' I smooth down my dress and pinch my cheeks for colour and open the door with a ready smile on my lips. I hadn't realised I was holding my breath and it comes out in one excited burst leaving me breathless as I fall into his arms crying.

'Karl, my goodness!' I pull away. I register his curly long hair and deep blue eyes. His denim shirt is drenched in a masculine and heavy scent. His skin is soft and there are tears in his eyes.

'Sandra, you look lovely. You're my big sister.' His voice is quiet and his accent is broad Essex. His arm is around my waist and he stares into my eyes as if looking for some familiarity.

'Come in. Come in.' I can't let go of his hand although it's calloused and rough. I wipe my laughing eyes noticing his are glistening too. I wipe mine with a tissue that I take from my sleeve hardly able to speak. 'It's like looking in the mirror.'

'You've my eyes alright. We must take after Mum,' he says.

'Mum,' I repeat. The name sounds funny on my lips. It's so weird to think he's speaking about the same woman - the stranger who gave birth to us - she wasn't my mum at all.

'Come in, we can't stand on the doorstep. You must need a coffee after that drive. How long did it take you?'

'Only a couple of hours.' He follows me inside.

'Tea, filter coffee or I can make a cappuccino or latte?'

'You're posh!' He laughs and I don't know if he's referring to my accent, my home or to the coffee. 'I grew up in a council flat,' he adds.

'You're so good to come all this way.' I had suggested we meet in a hotel half-way but he had insisted on making the whole journey.

I usher him into the living room but I can't take my eyes from his face. I'm trying to find shades of the likeness in our features or his demeanour and I'm still holding his hand thinking of the blue eyes we share. 'Do you think we look alike?' I ask.

His smile is wide and warm. 'Your nose is smaller and you haven't got my big chin. You're better looking all round,' he concludes.

I laugh and trace his stubble with my fingers. My tears are flowing freely and he pulls me to him again and we are laughing.

'I never thought this day would come,' he whispers.

It's been a long time since I've held a man in my arms other than my husband who spends most of his days sitting at a desk. In contrast Karl is strong and muscular and I like the reassuring feel of his warmth.

'Me neither. I can't quite believe it, Karl. Coffee?' His name is beginning to seem familiar on my lips.

'Sounds good, thank you.'

'Come in the kitchen with me?' I don't want to leave him alone. I have so many questions. I pop on the kettle and we smile at each other for what seems a long time then I shake my head. 'I'm all emotional, I'm sorry.'

He stands in the middle of the kitchen with his back against the counter. 'I feel the same, Sandra. It is a big deal. It's not every day you meet your big sister for the first time.'

'When the agency contacted me to say they'd found

you,' I reply. 'I couldn't believe it. I've looked for you for years but there was no trace and I never stopped hoping they'd find you…'

'We went to Scotland for over ten years but I hated it. We lived in the countryside, right up in the highlands but I'm a townie at heart. I like people. I like busy streets and places.' His eyes follow me around the kitchen. 'This is a lovely house, have you lived here long?'

'Since the girls were small so, I suppose, almost twenty years now.'

'And you have a son?'

'Ben. He's a lawyer.'

'Grandchildren?'

'Goodness, not yet,' I laugh. 'He's only just qualified.'

'Who looks after the garden? It's massive.'

'It's not so big - we have an old boy who helps us - he comes in once a week and cuts the lawn.'

I indicate for him to sit at the long table near the bi-fold doors that overlook the garden. We've had so many family meals at this table: birthdays, Easter lunches and Christmas and now Karl, my baby brother, is here in *my* home.

My hands are shaking and I feel silly smiling constantly at him but he shakes his head good-naturedly, as if it's the most normal thing in the world.

He takes three heaped spoons of sugar using the wet spoon to dip into the glass bowl. He stirs his coffee noisily and sloppily and it spills out of the China mug and over the table so I mop it up with a cloth.

He watches me and leans back against the chair with his arms folded. 'Were your parents rich?'

'They were quite well off - yes. And yours?'

'I grew up in a tower block where kids were injecting themselves at fifteen and smoking hash.'

'I'm sorry.' My smile fades. 'It must have been awful.'

He shrugs. 'I was lucky. I got out.'

'Did you marry?'

'For a few years. I've a boy of seventeen that I don't see and a baby with my new partner. I'm divorced. I wasn't a good role model for a number of years.'

'You don't see your son?'

He turns away. 'I was confused about relationships for a long time. It's better this way. But tell me about you. You have two daughters?' he adds brightly. 'It must have been lovely for them growing up here.'

'It was.' I watch him trying to see my home; the wooden oak floors, wide hallways, and expensive wood framed doors. I try to imagine my life through his eyes then I say, 'How lovely you're a carpenter. How did you get into that?'

He shrugs and slurps noisily from his mug. 'I couldn't find work for ages but then I made some shelves and bits and pieces. I trawled markets for stuff to do up and paint and sell on. And I found I had a knack for it and I enjoyed it. So bit by bit I started making stuff from scratch.'

'You sound as though you love it.'

'I do.' His eyes shine.

'I'm pleased you're happy, Karl.'

'I wasn't always. I found out I was adopted when I was sixteen and it was a shock. My parents were not getting on and my dad shouted that I wasn't his before he stormed out of the flat. I thought my mum had had an affair or something but she sat me down and told me the truth. They adopted me at four weeks. She told me my birth mother couldn't look after me, and that she was an addict and I'd been taken into care and so mum and dad adopted me. But dad had just left…' he sighs.

'It must have been difficult to find out like that. Such a shock.'

'It was. I went a bit crazy and dropped out of school and fell in with the wrong crowd. It wasn't a great time. I ended up getting this girl pregnant and then I left her and by the time I realised my mistake and went back it was too late. She'd lost the baby. She'd also met someone else and didn't want me in her life. So I fooled around a bit more and got married and when my son was born I was freaked out. I couldn't cope with the responsibility. I hadn't grown up myself…'

'How do you feel about that now?'

'She moved away and I haven't seen him since.'

'But you have a new baby.'

'Lilly, yes. She was the reason I went to the agency. I felt ready to find our mum.'

'What can you do about your son?'

'I hope the boy will come looking for me as I did when I went to find out about mum - our birth mother. I couldn't believe that you had been looking for me.'

'It wasn't easy to get any information. It's taken me years to find you.'

'I couldn't believe the agency were looking for me. I didn't even know I had a sister.'

'We've found each other Karl but mum's gone.' I lean over and take his big hand in mine.

'Yes.'

'They said she died of an overdose twenty years ago.'

He nods. 'We might have helped her had we found

her.'

'We are the age now that she was when she died,' I sigh. 'I understand her despair and how she must have felt.'

'You do?' he laughs. 'What do you know about drugs and hardship?'

'You'd be surprised.' I take my hand away and raise my coffee mug to my lips and he looks out of the window.

'What does your husband do?'

'Mark is a business analyst in the city.'

'So, not short of a bob or two. You're pretty much protected here aren't you. I imagine you've led a happy life?'

I nod. 'Yes. Very.'

'With all life's comforts; good schools, safe neighbourhood, foreign holidays, golf, horse riding lessons…?'

'Yes.'

'So how would you ever understand what our mother went through, what it was like to be thrown out of your home, pregnant and hanging out with the wrong crowd? How would you know what it's like to have no money and nowhere to live? You've only ever known luxury like this.' He laughs, 'You live in an ivory tower. You have no idea about hardship, fear, squalor or dirty lives.'

'Don't I?'

'Look at you. Your jewellery, the white grand piano in the living room, the coffee machine, the big fridge, cars on the drive and two garages - ordinary people don't live like this.'

'No.' I place my mug on the table.

His blue eyes are burning like they're on fire. 'Not

where I come from.'

'Are you angry that I was adopted into a wealthy family?'

'Not angry. But I wonder what it would have been like if you'd had my parents and I'd had yours. How would you have survived? What would you have done finding out at sixteen? How did they tell you?'

His coffee mug leaves wet rings on the wood and I wipe them away as I speak. 'They told me from a baby. They told me they'd chosen me deliberately. They told me how lucky they were to have me and I felt happy and blessed to be so loved.'

'You didn't need our mum. You didn't need a drug addict in your life. You didn't bother looking for her.'

'I was always curious but I didn't want to be disloyal to my own parents. When I searched for you they told me she had died.'

'How did you feel?'

'Sad, not to have known her.'

'Are your parents still alive?'

'Yes.'

'Do they know about me?'

'Of course, and they're very happy. They'd like to meet you.'

His shirt hangs out of the back of his jeans and he stands quietly at the glass door staring out into the September garden. The leaves are turning their magical autumn colours and the grass is damp from the rain overnight. I take out smoked salmon, prawns and filo pastry tarts and salad that I've prepared for our lunch and place them on the table thinking I should have cooked potatoes or baked bread.

He stares at the array of food on the table. 'We don't have a lot in common do we, Sandra?'

'We haven't had a chance to find out,' I reply handing him a napkin. My heart begins thumping and I'm upset by his tone.

He pulls out his wallet and takes out a photograph. When he turns it to face me there's a picture of a black girl with her baby. 'This is my partner, Iris.'

'That's a lovely photograph.'

'She has two other children with two other men.'

I stare silently at him.

'That shocks you doesn't it?'

'Not really.'

'Does it disgust you?'

'It makes me sad.'

He puts the photograph away silently and I wonder if he's disappointed with my answer so I say:

'There are so many children growing up in dysfunctional families and sometimes with no family at all. I consider myself lucky that we have a lovely family and I'm pleased you are here, Karl. Please help yourself. I hope you're hungry?'

He piles food onto his plate taking half of everything and begins to eat before I have served myself. He wipes mayonnaise from his mouth with the back of his hand.

'I could say you're a dysfunctional family,' he argues. 'All this isn't normal, is it? No-one has this. Are you happy?'

'Happy?' I repeat unnecessarily. 'I'm blessed to have two lovely daughters, and a hardworking son and a loving husband.'

'You've had everything on a plate, Sandra. You were

one of the lucky ones. I've had to scrimp and save and graft hard and even now my flat is only rented. We don't own it.'

'But you have a lovely daughter and a beautiful partner.'

'But I don't have any of this. We don't eat like this. We have pies and potatoes and jerk chicken and rice and pasta. Sometimes if I have a good week we get an Indian. We don't have these luxuries.' He eats quickly and with his mouth full, and I wonder how I can help him.

'Iris helps at the local shelter and sometimes I volunteer too. We try to help others less fortunate than us. Can I smoke in here?'

'If you like.' I hate smoking but it seems churlish not to let him. He is my brother. He lights up and blows a plume of smoke in he air.

I know the girls will smell it later so I stand up and open a window. Karl pushes his chair back from the table and sits with his legs sprawled.

'Would you like a dessert?'

'No.' He exhales another plume of smoke then takes another gulp of smoked air. His eyes are creased in a dark frown. 'Aren't you going to tell me they're bad for me?'

I smile. 'I'm your sister not your mother.'

His laugh is bitter. 'Are you disappointed?'

'With you or with myself?'

'I'm not what you were expecting am I?'

'I don't know.'

'Or hoping for?'

'I didn't hope. I was happy when I found you and of course, I was excited and curious to meet you.'

He stands up, takes a deep breath and lets out a long

sigh. 'Perhaps it was a mistake me coming here. We don't have much to say to each other and we have nothing in common. Maybe I'd better go.' The cigarette dangles from his lips as he tucks in his shirt.

'I was hoping you'd stay and meet the girls. They'll be home soon.'

'I'm probably not the best uncle. Not a great role model to have around.'

'You haven't given yourself much of a chance. Besides they'll never forgive me if I don't make you stay.'

'They're twins?'

'Yes.'

'I bet they're beautiful. Do they take after you with blue eyes and that wide smile?'

'See for yourself.' The front door opens and there's a cacophony of giggling and excited voices in the hallway as they call out.

'Hello..'

'Hi.'

'That's them. They're here. They're home.'

He scowls. 'I don't want to meet them. I'm not ready. They'll think I'm the poor relation. The bloke who speaks badly and stinks the house out with HIS fags.' He stubs his cigarette into a crumb-filled plate. 'I'll be inferior and they'll look down on me just as your sort always do. I'm what you call a tradesman. A handyman-'

'Jesus was a carpenter and you are my brother.' I put my hand on his arm.

'Jesus didn't have two illegitimate children and a black girlfriend.'

'No-one is perfect.'

The girls' voices fill the corridor and I hear the bubble

of their excitement as they close the front door, calling out and laughing.

'Anyone home?'

'Hi…'

'We're in the kitchen I call back.'

The door opens and my two gorgeous daughters are staring openly at Karl, smiling and happy to meet their uncle.

'Oh my god,' he whispers.

'This is Ellie and,' I move to stand beside the wheelchair. 'This is Samantha.'

Ellie's face lights up and she throws her arms around her uncle's neck. She hugs him hard then she leans down and says to her sister. 'This is our uncle Karl.'

Ellie is still holding her uncle's hand and she pulls him closer to the wheelchair.

Samantha's face is filled with excitement and her brown eyes are so pure, innocent and sweet that it brings tears to my eyes.

Beside me, Karl is visibly moved. He smiles at Ellie and then bends down to speak to her twin. But Samantha can't see him. She was born blind. A lack of oxygen at birth caused her to be brain damaged.

I put my arm around Ellie and hug her tightly. She's studying to be a nurse at the local college and she works at the hospital. On her day off she looks after Samantha, as she's always done. They are twins after all.

When Karl looks up his eyes are filled with pain and I put my hand on his shoulder to reassure him. I can't tell him that their mother didn't want a disabled child or that I could never have adopted one without the other but I will one day.

Ellie says to me. 'Have you had a lovely time together, Mum? Did you catch up on all those missing years?'

'We will, my darling. Everything takes time…'

Karl stands up and pulls me into a hug. His lips are twitching as he holds his emotion in check but he can't stop the tears escaping down his cheek. 'I'm sorry. I thought you had…had it all.'

'I do, now that you are in our life. We have it all.'

Samantha's pronunciation, although very slow, is better that it used to be. 'Can we meet your baby?' she asks.

Karl bends down and places his hand on hers. Kneeling beside him, I brush away his tears with my fingers. When he replies his voice is a hoarse whisper. 'I'd like that very much.'

Letters Abroad

Mijas, Spain
12th October 2002

Dear Mr Stevens,
Please find the enclosed photograph that I came upon by chance. It was wedged in the drawer where I keep the playing cards and games. I assume that by some oversight it was popped away by mistake and I thought you would like me to return it.

I would also like to take this opportunity to thank you for the work that you and your brother did on my villa. It was such a pleasant surprise to return and find that the gutter of the villa is now fixed and that you took such wonderful care of my garden. I was very nervous renting out my house for two months to two complete strangers whilst I was visiting my daughter in Australia but I can happily say that now, I have no regrets whatsoever.

I do hope that you enjoyed the summer and that your

brother is fully recovered.

Regards,
Susan Loftborough

P.S. I hope you don't mind me mentioning that the lady in the photograph looks remarkably like a woman I often see in the village. She has coffee alone most days on the terrace of a little Spanish bar overlooking the bay of Fuengirola.

London, England
6th November 2002

Dear Mrs Loftborough,
Thank you very much for your recent letter and the photograph. We thoroughly enjoyed our stay on the Coast. I miss Peter enormously. He felt so happy and well in the last few months that he had with me. He loved your beautiful garden and sat happily for hours under the shade of a tree reading which gave him great pleasure. As both of us were recently divorced we enjoyed the solitude and, may I say, took refuge in your wonderful home.

I still remember the intoxicating smells from your garden on a warm summer evening as we sipped wine and played cards on the terrace. I do hope that the pink bougainvillea that we planted beside the front door is flourishing and that you didn't think it a liberty that we felt so at home.

Thank you again.

Yours,
John Stevens

P.S. The lady in the photograph often sat in the small bar. We formed a brief friendship with her during our stay.

Mijas, Spain
12th December, 2002

Dear John Stevens,
I was so terribly sorry when I received your letter with the sad news about Peter. I hardly know what to write but I can only say I understand your pain having lost my husband three years ago. I am still unsure of my plans but do hope to return to Australia soon - perhaps at Easter. I would think of renting my villa – should you feel like returning here.

The bougainvillea that you planted is such a vivid and pretty colour. I sometimes want to touch it to reassure myself that it is real. It is such a welcoming sight and although we never met, I often think of you and Peter when I come home.

I hope you don't think it inappropriate that I enclose a Christmas card and wish you much happiness for 2003.

Kind Regards,

Susan

P.S. Several weeks ago I saw the lady from your photograph and I plucked up the courage to speak to her. We have met several times since then. For some unknown reason, I didn't mention Peter. I didn't want to intrude.

Cayman Islands
3rd January 2003

Dear Susan

I hope it is not too late to wish you the very best of luck and health for this year. I decided at the last minute to spend Christmas and New Year in the Caribbean with my two children even though they are teenagers and I don't see much of them! When I took early retirement to care for Peter I never imagined I would be so lucky as to be able to jet away at the last minute. I return to London next week.

With regard to your offer of the villa I would be very interested in returning to the Costa del Sol. Please let me know if you are going to Australia so that I may check on the flights and leave my flat in London in order. I would hate to return after a few months and find the bills haven't been paid!

Yours, Steven

P.S. I am pleased that you have spoken to Joyce. Peter

didn't want to tell her that he was ill.

Mijas, Spain
31st January, 2003

Dear John

I can barely contain my excitement. My daughter Sally has invited me over to Sydney again – for SIX months! I am so thrilled and can hardly think what to pack, even though I am not leaving until 30th March. I can't wait to see my grandchildren; Joshua and Kelly. They are now six and eight. Sally and Jonathan both work too hard and at least if I am there with them, I feel I can help!

The villa will be free for six months. I can leave the key with the neighbours as I did the last time. It might sound sentimental but I would be so happy if you could look after my home. Would it sound silly to think of you as a good friend even though we have never met?

Love, Susan

P.S. I haven't mentioned to Joyce about your visit. But she did mention that you and Peter look so much alike. I didn't realise you were identical twins – she said she could barely tell the two of you apart!

London, England
28th February 2003

Dear Susan

I think your excitement must be contagious. When I
received your letter I could barely contain my delight at
the thought of returning to somewhere so lovely. I should
certainly like to take the villa from the beginning of April
and stay as long as possible.

It is such a task wondering what to bring for so long so I
can understand how difficult it must be for you, going all
that way!

I'll arrange payment for the villa as I did last year – I
have added a further ten percent on the rent – I hope you
find that fair for both of us.

Love John

P.S. Perhaps it would be better if you say nothing to
Joyce about my visit. I will tell Joyce in person about Peter.
They became very close.

Sydney, Australia.
10th May 2003

My Dear John

I hope you found my note about the tomato plants. I
left the canes and larger pots for you to transfer them into
when they get a bit bigger. They're in the shed - if you

haven't found them already.

I cannot begin to tell you how different life is here. It's amazing how quickly you can slip so easily into other people's countries and lives!

Sally is working part-time now which means she has more time with the children after school. Jonathan continues to work hard at the bank but seems happy doing so. And I have taken up painting! Would you believe that the teacher in my art class says I have a natural talent for it – so funny to think that this flair has lain buried for these past 68 years! Anyway I am discovering my new self and meeting lots of people.

I hope you are happy in the villa again. I often like to picture you pottering in the garden. Perhaps I might sketch a portrait of how I think you might look – or would that be terribly rude of me?

Lots of love, Susan

P.S. Say hello to Joyce. We became quite good friends during the past few months even though she must be nearly twenty years younger than me.

Mijas, Spain
12th July 2003

Dear Susan
It seems so strange for me to be sitting at your table, drinking a glass of chilled wine and smelling the beautiful

jasmine. It is so pleasant here. Your peaceful home is like a quiet sanctuary amid the noise and haste of the rest of the world.

The tomato plants have just produced their first 'offspring' - I will share them with Joyce at dinner tonight.

I feel now that I must tell you what happened last summer. I will be brief but please don't think me of cold heart or devoid of emotion.

During our visit last year both Peter and I fell in love with Joyce and to say that I wasn't upset when they formed a relationship would be a lie. I was embarrassed and distraught that the jealousy from our youth had re-emerged in our adult life and I became upset and angry with Peter. I felt he held no regard for Joyce and her emotions. And I told him so. But, he only wanted to live life at the end and to feel loved once more.

I wonder now, if Peter hid the photograph surreptitiously in the drawer or if it was a coincidence. But when you wrote to me, I knew then that I must return. I can only say now that I haven't felt this happy for a very long time and am trying to persuade Joyce to return with me to England.

With love, John

P.S. Joyce sends you much love.

Sydney, Australia
15th September 2003

* * *

My Dear John,

Sally has asked me to move here! I cannot tell you how happy I am to be with my only daughter. I will be selling the villa. Please write and say that you will buy it.

Must dash to my art class. Will forward the portrait of you soon – which should hopefully, make you and Joyce both laugh!

Much love as always, Susan x

Cayman Islands
3rd January 2004

Dear Susan

Thank you for the painting. Fortunately I am only the shadow in the background and you have captured your garden perfectly. We hope you like the enclosed photograph. It was a small wedding and I was pleased my children were with me but we missed you.

We look forward to meeting up in Mijas at Easter to sign the documents on the villa. We will have much to celebrate.

All our love, Joyce and John xx

Aqua Tofana

Michael looks over the the balcony of the dress circle and
sees them instantly. They're mingling with the crowd,
finding their seats; third row from the front. The tall man
has hunched shoulders and short white hair. His wife is
lithe, blonde and glamorous. They make a gracious couple
as they stand and smile to let another couple pass.

The orchestra begins tuning, thumping out of sync,
horns and trumpets, timpani and strings. A cacophony of
random notes like Michael's heartbeat.

Gradually the audience settles and the orchestra is
silent, lights are dimmed and someone coughs. Then
curtains part to reveal the garden of the Commendatore,
and a figure on the stage appears to be watching a house.
Don Giovanni appears and Mozart's music fills the
auditorium.

Michael bites his top lip and his hands begin to shake.
He strains his neck to get a better view of the couple in
the audience. Her blond hair catches the lights. She is
engrossed in the performance.

It would be their last opera together.

It is her curtain call. Her finale. Her last night.

The first few minutes of the opera absorbs all Michael's concentration even though he's not thinking about the performance on stage. He breathes using his diaphragm, controlling his nerves and shaking hands. His heart rate decreases and eventually his breathing returns to normal. He's always loved the stage; theatre and opera. Music carries him into a dreamless time and to a world where he can escape, where he can be anyone.

He blinks. He mustn't lose himself tonight. He must maintain his fake identity. At least until the end of his performance. He smooths his black skirt against his thighs and crosses his legs. The unfamiliar breasts push against his satin blouse and he touches the back of his head reassuringly and the unfamiliar dark wig.

Don Attavio's tenor voice and Donna Anna's soprano fills the Gaiety. Michael knows the theatre well. It was built in 1871. It's one of Dublin's most prestigious venues with a beautiful Venetian façade. Where he sits in the dress circle, there are sixteen private boxes and tiers. Above him are the Grand and Upper Circles. The Baroque style appears exotic and rich and he'd read that the last refurbishment had cost nine and a half million euros.

He fingers the small vial in his skirt pocket. Four to six drops is enough to deliver a painless death in a few hours. At least his victim will die in elegant surrounds.

'Fuggi, crudele fuggi.' *Flee, cruel one, flee*, they sing, and Michael is filled with courage. It's too late for his target. It's too late for her to flee.

Her fate is sealed.

Along with his younger sister Anna, Michael was ten-years-old when he dressed up for the first time. They giggled excitedly, raiding their mother's clothes; high-heeled shoes, scarves and blouses. They scattered colourful satins, crepes and cottons around the bedroom before finally adding make-up to their baby faces.

They were discovered by his mother and her friend. They laughed indulgently and admired their naughty creativity but after the friend had gone his mother's smile had frozen. She had slapped him repeatedly, calling him a poof and a faggot. Finally she whipped him into the corner of the bedroom where he cowered away from her beating. His skin turning brownish shades of purple.

It wasn't until years later that Michael realised his mother had married above herself. She had seduced his father, a well-to-do bank manager and merged into the upper classes hiding her accent as carefully as she accentuated her beauty but she was unable to suppress her abusive nature and violent roots.

To the outside world they were a happy couple. His mother was funny, tolerant and kind but at home she was a bully and a tyrant.

When Michael was fourteen he wanted to take the part of Prospero in the school play but his mother had been furious.

'I don't care if you want to be Macbeth, Shylock or even Jesus Christ – you're not feckin' dressing up. It's time you behaved like a man. Get yourself a girlfriend. Get laid for heaven's sake.'

Michael's father, who adored the opera, remained silent as he did with most things in his life. While opera was his passion and drinking was his refuge his wife found other outlets for her ardour. She had various affairs and regularly took out her frustration by tormenting her children.

Over the years Michael recognised his father's meekness and one night it dawned on him that his children meant little to him. When Anna was thirteen she came home from the cinema with a friend but she'd stumbled in the street and broken the heel of her plastic shoe. Their mother had dragged her into the kitchen saying she would glue it together but as the door slammed closed he heard her raised voice.

Fear turned Michael rigid.

'You're a slut! You've been taking your clothes off. Who is he?' his mother shouted. 'You're a feckin' tramp. A tart.'

Michael heard the first slap of skin then the heavy wallop of his mother's hand and Anna screamed. She tried to deny the accusations and was sobbing hysterically but this only enraged their mother. Michael turned to his father and pulled on his arm.

'You've got to help,' he cried. But his father pushed him away and went into the lounge where he poured whisky into a Waterford crystal glass and turned up the volume of Verdi's, *Hebrew Slave Chorus*.

In the Gaiety, Giovanni's baritone voice rings out with the champagne aria, 'Fin ch'han dal vin' and Michael catches his breath at the richness of Don Giovanni's tone.

When Anna was fifteen she stopped eating. She was malnourished and had a sickly pallor. Her arms and legs were like sticks so Michael developed an interest in cooking. He thought that if he could tempt her to eat then she would get better so he began cooking, making succulent fish dishes, experimenting with vegetarian recipes and perfecting his presentation so the food was tempting and irresistible.

One day he baked sultana scones, caramel and chocolate tray bakes and skinny cheese straws but then his mother arrived home.

'Get out of my kitchen,' she shouted. 'I'm not having a bloody fairy baking in my kitchen. Out you feckin' faggot!' she screamed, and catching him a surprise blow to the side of his head he had fallen back against the door frame. His nose bleeding Michael went to retaliate and he lifted his fist but his father pulled his arm away.

'You're better than her,' he whispered.

'Why don't you ever do something?' he hissed.

But his father's eyes glazed over and without saying another word he left the room.

Now the actors are in the ballroom. Don Giovanni leads Zerlina off stage to rape her while Leporello distracts her boyfriend Masetto. When Zerlina cries for help Don Giovanni tries to fool the onlookers by dragging Leporello into the room and accuses him of seducing Zerlina.

The audience are silent. Not a cough or sweet wrapper is unfurled.

A few months ago when his father was working in London, Michael returned home unexpectedly. He opened the front door and Bobby, Anna's new boyfriend, was standing in the hallway. He was tucking his shirt hurriedly into his jeans. His eyes were dark and wild.

'You're mother's a slapper.' He pushed past Michael and ran out of the house laughing.

Michael found his mother in the lounge buttoning her blouse, looking dishevelled, red-faced and slightly drunk.

'What happened?' he asked and when she didn't reply, he asked. 'Where's Anna?'

With an unsteady hand his mother poured red wine into a dirty glass, spilling blood-red drops onto the carpet. 'She's asleep,' she slurred.

'What happened with Bobby?'

'What dutink?' his mother leered.

'He's Anna's boyfriend.'

'He's a real man,' she taunted. 'He's a proper Don Juan. Not like you or your father. He wanted me.' She stabbed her chest with her thumb and shouted. 'And I wanted sex – and God it was good!'

Michael realised then just how far she would go to destroy all their lives.

It is almost time for the interval. Michael slips out from his aisle seat and makes his way to the bar where uniformed waiters are polishing glasses and waiting for the interval onslaught. Keeping his eyes downcast Michael starts at the near-end noting names of the pre-booked drinks along the shelf. He eliminates clusters of more than two glasses but there are so many he can't read the names quickly enough. The theatre doors open and people surge around him collecting their drinks. His heart thumps louder. He would have to be quick. Panicking, muttering his surname, over and over, reading names, then suddenly he sees it.

Orrisey, the 'M' was smeared on the flimsy paper:

One red wine and one whisky. He glances over his shoulder. The white hair of his father weaving through the crowd toward him.

Michael fumbles.

His father is close. He is almost-

Michael's shaking fingers takes the vial from his pocket. He quickly tips the contents into the wine glass.

'Excuse me, Miss,' his father's voice is close to his ear. He reaches over Michael's shoulder and takes the glasses.

Michael ducks away inhaling his father's familiar aftershave. He steps aside holding onto his wig, his heart palpitating furiously. He walks unsteadily to lean with his shoulder against a cold wall pretending to be absorbed in the programme, swallowing repeatedly, hardly daring to watch his parents.

His mother flashes a smile at a passing stranger. She takes her first sip.

Michael holds his breath.

She sips again, then again. It seems an eternity until she's drained her glass.

The bells rings.

His father places their empty glasses on the nearby shelf.

In the early seventeenth century, Giula Tofana had sold her poison to over six hundred people. Those who died were invariably husbands of unhappy wives. There had even been unfounded rumours that Mozart might have been poisoned using Agua Tofana.

Michael hangs back long enough to collect her glass. Then he mixes with the crowd and files back to his seat. From his vantage point in the dress circle he watches his mother. She places the programme across her knees and the curtains part.

Listening to Zerlina's soprano, 'Batti, batti, o bel Masetto' - *Beat me, beat me, o dear Masetto* - Michael imagines the poison: arsenic, lead and belladona sliding through his mother's veins. A colourless, tasteless liquid that mixes easily with wine. She would begin to feel hot, develop a headache and feel dizzy.

Death would be quick.

On stage the actors gathered outside Elvira's house where Leporello threatens to leave Giovanni. His master attempts to calm him with a peace offering of money and they sing the duet, 'Eh via buffone' - *Come on, buffoon.*

Michael watches his mother as she raises her programme and begins to fan her face. She leans forward and slides her jacket from her shoulders.

Michael watches and waits.

After the final scene he stands with the audience to applaud. Below him his mother does not rise from her seat.

He must get back to the hospital. Since Anna's attempted suicide he has hardly left her side. She is making slow progress but the damage she suffered at her mother's hand has been profound.

Now, at last, their past has been vindicated.

He takes one last look around the majestic theatre and then straightening his skirt he makes his exit, head bowed, out into the darkness of Dublin's crowded streets. As he walks he whistles, shedding his disguise, tossing his wig, his jacket and his skirt into various trash bins along his haphazard route knowing the items will be picked up by the homeless sleeping on the streets.

Nearing the hospital he pulls a long jacket from his bag. He hums the *Champagne Aria* and when he sings he's reminded of Gary who he met on a catering course a year ago. They became friends, then lovers. He understood Michael immediately. He knew the hurt, frustration and anger that seethed inside him and Gary had been positive, kind and supportive.

One night, laying in the darkness of their bedroom with the moon glowing though the shutters, Michael had confided in Gary.

'I need to do something.'

'It's not worth it,' Gary had replied. 'You must let it go.'

'I can't,' Michael had whispered. 'I just can't do that.'

In a dark alleyway Michael tosses the last piece of evidence into a bin where it smashes into smithereens, shattering his past into tiny shards of sharp glass.

Tonight Gary was his alibi. Together they will protect Anna and get her well again.

Michael was determined. The past was now behind them. They would all live happily ever after.

A Pair Of Shoes

Gail let herself into the house as she'd done every Saturday but now she couldn't believe she'd spent the whole summer abroad, in the sunshine. As she opened the door she couldn't believe she'd been away for five months.

Now she was back. She felt different. Older? Wiser?

Even the neighbourhood seemed to have changed. The streets seemed a little bit wider, the few trees on the pavement a little greener and the houses a little smaller.

She was surprised her sister's house looked slightly drab and the garden needed weeding.

Filled with excitement, she called out from the back door.

'Monica?' she laughed, 'I'm home!'

'I'm here - in the lounge.' Monica jumped to her feet, sweeping three-year old Alfie from the floor and into her arms. 'Look who's here. Auntie Gail's home.'

The girls met in the hallway and Alfie was squeezed between them as they hugged. A tumble of words fell from their lips like marbles bouncing down the staircase.

'Look at the colour of you!'

'Your hair has grown!'

'I've put on weight!'

'Not as much as me.'

'You're so tanned.'

'Oh Alfie, aren't you so adorable.' Gail took him in her arms and smothered his face in tiny kisses making him giggle. 'Haven't you grown up, little one?'

'I'll pop the kettle on,' said Monica moving into the kitchen. 'We can have a glass of wine after we've put Alfie to bed. He's been so desperate to see you I couldn't take him up just yet.'

Gail carried Alfie expertly on her hip and smiled indulgently into his blue eyes while surreptitiously watching her sister move around the kitchen. She seemed different: slower, lethargic, tired. Or was it something else?

Monica carried their mugs into the lounge and the girls sat beside each other on the sofa. Alfie took up most of their attention, chatting intermittently, as he pulled a book, a truck and finally a teddy onto Gail's lap. Then he curled up for a cuddle and some special kisses from his Auntie.

'So, where's the handsome hunk?' Gail smiled at her sister and gave her a slow, knowing, wink.

'Showering. He's going out with the boys tonight. You look fabulous, Gail - bumming around the Greek islands really suited you.'

'I was born to travel.' Gail's eyes were bright and alive with excitement. Her tanned skin only emphasised her piercing blue eyes and once again Monica was reminded that her younger sister was the prettier, slimmer and funnier of the two and she shifted her legs uncomfortably under the weight of her body on the sofa.

'I want to hear all about it…'

'Monica, honey?' Heavy footsteps bound down the stairs. 'Have you seen my- oh my God, Gail? Is it really you? Welcome back, stranger…'

Gail leaned forward with Alfie still in her arms and she wrapped one arm around Neil's neck for a hug.

Monica watched him as he kissed Gail's cheek. They looked like an ideal couple; tall, blond with muscular shaped bodies and they held hands as they smiled at each other.

'Alfie's grown.'

'He's a little boy now,' Neil agreed ruffling the boy's head.

'You look lovely, Gail.' Then he turned his attention to Monica. 'I'm in a hurry, sweetie, have you seen my leather jacket?'

'It's on the back of the chair in the kitchen, where you left it.'

'Thanks, baby.' He bent to kiss her cheek and spicy cologne she'd bought him for his birthday hung like an invisible cloud around his head. 'I'll see you later, honey. You two have a good catch up.'

They listened to him in the kitchen and when the back door banged shut Monica said. 'Come on Alfie. It's way past your bedtime. We've a lot to catch up on.'

Alfie's eyes were closing when the sisters took him up to the bedroom, chatting and fussing quietly over him. Even though he was almost asleep Gail read to him, savouring the sweet moment while Monica tidied the bedroom. After fifteen minutes they were back downstairs and pouring a glass of chilled Pinot Grigio from the fridge.

'Cheers!' They tapped glasses and giggled.

'It's been a long time.'

'Too long.'

'So, Neil's gone out with his mates to give us time to catch up?'

'I've made a shepherd's pie. It'll be ready in twenty minutes.' Monica didn't say that Neil was out most Saturday nights now and sometimes during the week. It was too early for that conversation. 'So, tell me all about your holiday.'

'It was fantastic. I can understand how foreigners want to live over there and work in bars and restaurants. It's such a completely different way of life.'

'Did you meet anyone special?' Monica laid knives and forks on the table. 'Costas? Stavros? Mykonos?'

'That's an island, silly,' Gail laughed. 'I did meet someone who was quite special. Loukas - he was - quite different.'

'Only quite special?'

'Well.. yes. I mean, it's not like you and Neil. Loukas didn't sweep me off my feet. He wasn't muscular and handsome and well, you know, lovely…like Neil.'

'But you fancied him?'

'He made me laugh.'

'That's the main thing.'

'And he was kind.'

'That's important.'

'But he wasn't thoughtful like Neil.'

Monica stared at her sister. 'Neil, thoughtful?'

'Yes. You know, you told me how Neil brings you flowers each Saturday and how he came home early once to pick Alfie up from nursery classes – and do you remember that time you were in the park and you said Alfie was cold and Neil went and bought him a new jacket?'

'We weren't living together then.' Monica took the pie out of the oven, picked up a spoon and dug into the crispy potato topping and served large helpings.

Gail refilled their glasses. 'Weren't you?'

'Neil only moved in ten months ago.'

'Really? It seems longer.' Monica seemed lost in thought so Gail continued. 'He was so kind after Richard left you.'

Monica didn't reply. Instead she ate silently without looking up.

'Have you seen Richard? Has he been in touch?'

'No.'

'I can't believe he doesn't want to see his own son. Poor Alfie.'

'He doesn't want the responsibility.'

Gail sipped her wine. 'But Alfie is so…oh, I don't know gorgeous.'

'Let's not go on about the past. I want to hear all your news. So, what did you get up to with Loukas?'

'I met him on Aegina. I was wandering around the harbour and I thought he was a fisherman, but he'd borrowed the boat from a friend.' She pulled out her phone and flicked through photographs and hesitated at snapshot memories.

'You didn't put any of him on Facebook?' Monica said.

'He's not particularly good looking.' Gail turned the phone around and Monica peered at the screen.

'Are you in love with him?'

'I don't know.'

Monica squinted at the screen. 'His eyes are too close together and I'm not sure about the ponytail but so long as he is nice to you, that's the main thing.' She handed the phone back.

'I know but-'

Monica held up the palm of her hand then placed her knife and fork together on the empty plate.'Please don't say he's not like Neil - again.'

'I won't, but it's just that I've never seen anyone so in love. You know, like you when you met Neil you lit up. You were so depressed, Richard had just walked out and you were struggling to bring up Alfie on your own and Neil was there for you.'

Monica placed her hand over her wine glass to stop Gail refilling her glass. 'I'll be up at six again with Alfie. I'd better take it easy.'

Gail filled her own glass. 'Neil is just so wonderful with everyone.'

'That's a slight exaggeration.'

'It's just that when you and Neil met – it was so special. He couldn't take his eyes off you – let alone his hands. You laughed all the time and you had fun. Do you remember how you took Alfie to the swimming pool for the first time, together – you didn't stop laughing.'

'Are you in love with Loukas?'

'It's not like real love-'

'How do you know?'

'Well, with you and – well, with you I could see how happy you were. Neil is attentive. He makes you feel special-'

'Isn't Loukas like that?'

'He's more laid back. He won't put himself out. Like,

one day I didn't fancy going across the island to look at another bloody Greek temple so I said I'd prefer to stay on the beach – and Loukas just said okay, and went off on his own.'

'That's good.'

'No! It wasn't good, Monica. I wanted him to stay with me, not go sailing off to another island.'

'But you've got to be true to yourself. There's no point in trying to please someone – let alone you,' Monica teased.

'But Neil would have stayed with you. He wouldn't have gone sailing. He would have put you first.'

'Not necessarily.'

'He would. Don't you remember the time we were going to the cinema and he wanted to see that action movie but he came to see Hotel Marigold with us?'

'That was before he moved in.'

'Neil is like that – he idolises you and Alfie.'

Monica sighed. 'He might have done before.'

'What do you mean?'

Monica shrugged. 'Things change.' She stood up and began to place the dirty plates in the dishwasher. 'I'll just go and check on Alfie.'

When Monica came downstairs Gail was sitting in the lounge with her legs curled under her and a fresh glass of wine in her hand.

'What's changed?' she asked.

Monica pretended she didn't understand the question.

'Come on? Talk to me. What's happened?' Gail insisted.

'Nothing.'

'Has Neil changed?'

Monica shrugged, sat in the armchair and folded her legs under her bottom.

'Well, has he?'

'He's bound to – it was bound to happen.'

'Are you still in love?'

'Not like before. Things change,' Monica added.

Gail stared at her. Monica had everything. She had a beautiful baby and a handsome boyfriend, yet she was never happy. Gail would swap her life in a heartbeat for Monica's. Even as bad as Richard had been to Monica, Gail knew she would have been different with him. She would have coaxed out his softer side and his gentler nature. She would have looked after Richard.

'So what's wrong with Neil?'

'Nothing's wrong with him - people change.'

'Is it because he knows Alfie isn't his son? Does that make a difference? Do you want children together?' It's what Gail would have wanted had she been in Monica's shoes.

'I'm not ready for another child, Gail. I've got enough on my plate besides, I need to feel more… stable.'

'Stable?' Gail laughed. 'You've got a stud between the sheets and you're talking stable…'

'It's not always about that - although the sex has changed too.'

'Don't tell me, he's no longer the stallion he was?'

'I guess when you live together, you get into some sort of…routine. It's not make-believe any more. It's not all fun and laughter. There's the practical side of life, getting up, going to work, washing, dressing and feeding Alfie so things are bound to change.'

'But you do still fancy him? Don't you?'

Monica laughed. 'God, yes of course but…'

'But what? Monica – he's gorgeous. I know him. He's a lovely guy.'

'He's changed.' Monica blinked and wiped tears away with the back of her hand.

'How? He seemed just the same tonight.'

'I know. But it's the detail. All those lovely things he used to do have just fallen away. It's like he doesn't care any more.'

'Have you spoken to him about it?'

'Of course but he doesn't understand. He doesn't see it – or doesn't want to.'

'How has he changed?'

'All those small things that he did, you know the little things you talked about and the ones you remember, well – now he's stopped doing them.'

'Why?'

'I think it is my fault. I used to say things like Richard never took me out for dinner or Richard never bought me chocolates and so Neil always did it. It was like he was trying to make up for Richard and he wanted to prove he was better than Richard. So, he did nice things. Like that time when he bought Alfie that jacket - I was in tears that day – he was so kind.'

'Isn't he kind now?'

'He's not unkind. There is a difference.'

Gail sipped her wine and listened.

'The magic disappears,' Monica continued, 'That initial euphoria that we had when we were in love - goes. It vanished - poof - just like that.' She clicked her fingers. 'And it won't come back.'

'Maybe it will? Maybe it's just a phase.'

Monica shook her head. 'Before he moved in, he was always putting Alfie and me, first. It was always what we wanted and I thought this is how it would always be. I felt wanted again. I felt loved and important. Neil made me feel so special…'

'He doesn't any more?'

'No.'

'And sex?'

Monica shook her head. 'It used to be amazing; experimental and fun but now it's as if we've done it all so we can't be bothered.'

'Maybe you should buy something sexy? You're too young not to have a sex life.'

'We still do it – but the magic has gone. All the little things I like he seems to have forgotten about.'

'Then remind him,' Gail said with passion fuelled by Pinot Grigio.

'That's not the worst thing though.'

Gail stared at her sister's sad face wondering what could be worse. There was only one thing and her heart dropped with realisation. 'Oh, no.'

'Yesterday, it happened yesterday. I was getting ready to go to work and getting ready to take Alfie to the nursery. I was late and Alfie was running around being naughty. He wouldn't put on his coat or his shoes. It took me ages to get hold of him and get him ready-'

'And?' Gail passed Monica a tissue.

'Neil just sat playing on his iPhone.'

'So?'

'Before he would have helped me. He would have helped Alfie get his coat on and he would have tied his shoe laces but he didn't bother. He just sat doing what he wanted to do. I know Alfie isn't his but-'

'You think he's having an affair?'

Monica looked confused then hurt. 'Of course not, silly! He still loves me but don't you understand? He didn't even put Alfie's shoes on.'

Gail laughed. 'Thank goodness that's all it was.'

Monica shook her head. She had forgotten just how frustrating Gail could be. She really had no idea what it was like having a serious relationship. It was complicated. The real world was a bad, hard place and Gail seemed to sail through it without a worry in the world with no commitments and no responsibility.

If only the shoe had been on the other foot.

If only she was the one who'd travelled around Greece.

Monica would love to have sailed to every island. She would adore that freedom with Loukas or without him. Instead of living here with all the responsibility of a son, a mortgage and a man who paid her less and less attention.

'You don't understand, Gail.' Monica dabbed her eyes. 'It's all changed. It's just not the same.'

'For God's sake, Monica. It was just a pair of shoes.'

Something Might Happen

Sonia Brooks unfolded the creased newspaper and with a purple nail she ran her finger under the text, re-reading the obituary. Just to be sure. She didn't want to arrive too late or too early. She'd taken an early bus to Whitstable and it was a pretty town – she might even have lunch afterwards.

She replaced the Canterbury Times in the navy bag on her lap and stared out of the window. The bus rattled along and as it dropped down the hill to the town she could see the sea and the wind farm on the horizon.

How lovely that would be to wake up each morning to look at the changing tide and to walk along the slopes in Tankerton. So different to her life in the busy city that seemed to get more and more polluted.

She imagined Milton Lawson who died peacefully, he was 72, living here. She thought about his home and his family and she imagined them all and their grief. Funerals were such sad affairs.

She opened her compact and checked her appearance

licking the tip of her finger and wiping a smudge of mascara from under her large eyes. She added concealer to the spot on her chin and added pink lipstick.

Her iPhone was already set to Maps and she checked the distance she would have to walk from the bus stop in the centre of town. She was used to searching for information, after all, she had been on enough dating websites and met various men in different bars. She was quite independent but at thirty year-old she knew her body clock was ticking louder than the baby crying at the back of the bus.

Sonia glanced at the newspaper. Devoted husband to Stella and Dad to Mark, Iain, Freddie and Jenny. Sadly missed by family and friends and remembered as a teacher and historian. He was a scholar - a learned man - and Sonia had respect for anyone who had an education or who had done well in life. He was also respected in the local community and that was essential for Sonia. She would like to marry a man like Milton; tall, handsome, broad-shouldered with a sense of humour. Someone who knew things, not like some of the men she had dated who could barely string a sentence together or drank beer as if the world was coming to an end that very night. It was hard to find a man who, like her own father, opened doors for a lady to pass though first, or who always walked on the outside of the pavement to protect her from cars and puddle splashes but she wouldn't give up trying.

Sonia crossed her ankles pleased with her outfit. A navy dress with pink and purple flowers, high heels, and a jacket that matched the blue coral necklace at her throat.

The bus rattled through the town and the baby squealed louder. She stood up, dinged the bell and made her way gingerly downstairs, hanging onto the rail, tottering on high heels and swinging onto the ground floor. She was jolted as the bus came to a halt and she set her hat straight remembering the instruction.

Milton had requested: 'No flowers or funeral black.'

The High Street was busy and it took Sonia seven minutes to walk to the church. On the way she wondered if she would recognise anyone. It had been a long time since she had been to this area. She followed a couple toward the tree-lined pathway to the porch of the church. Once inside she quickly scanned the pews wondering where it would be best to sit. Not too near the front and certainly not at the back. The aisle was perfect. There was a space beside an elderly lady so she slid in to the seat and gazed up at the statue and crossed herself.

The old lady beside her returned her sad smile then glanced at the Order of Service. Milton had aged well; receding grey hair, spectacles and still a twinkle in his eye. It was a lovely photograph and she guessed Stella must have chosen it from one of the family selection.

Soft music played and Sonia glanced up at the church organ wondering what it was called. She looked at the old lady beside her who seemed lost in thought but looked up when she felt Sonia's gaze.

'What a beautiful piece of music,' Sonia whispered. 'Do you know it?'

'Adagio in G Minor,' the old lady replied.

'So beautiful.'

'Milton loved it.'

Sonia smiled. 'He did like music. Do you know the family well?'

The old lady slid a little closer as more footsteps clicked

down the aisle and new arrivals sat down.

'We taught together.'

'How lovely.'

'Yes but it was a long time ago now-'

'Was that at St Joseph's?'

The old lady frowned. 'No, no, it was at St Bart's.'

'Oh yes, of course, I always get those muddled up. How's Stella taking it?'

'It was a shock of course. But Jenny and the boys have been wonderful… so supportive.'

'Didn't Jenny get married?'

'Yes, years ago now.' She nods at the front row. 'They're her two boys Gavin and Edmund.'

Sonia looked at the family. Jenny's dark hair contrasted with her blond husband. 'The boys look like Milton's side of the family.'

'Do you think so?' The old lady craned her neck to see. 'I don't see it myself.'

'Well, it's been a long time since I saw any of them. Didn't Freddie go abroad?'

'No? I don't think so. He's up in London. Although he may have gone away before he went to medical school…'

'Maybe it was Mark then, I've always muddled them up.'

The old lady smiled. 'It's easy to do. Although I've always though Iain was more like his father-'

The music stopped. The door banged and the congregation fell silent.

Sonia turned around as a tall man in a crumpled suit strode down the aisle to the front. When Jenny looked up she smiled in surprise, jumped to her feet and threw her arms around his neck. Her husband shook the man's hand

and he greeted their two boys by ruffling their hair. Sonia thought he might sit with them but he didn't. He stood confidently at the front of the church with his hands in his pockets staring around. He nodded and smiled at a few guests then his eyes rested on Sonia and she could feel the heat of his stare, so she smiled and looked quickly down at Milton's face in her hand.

'Goodness Mark has come home,' the old lady whispered.

'That's a surprise,' agreed Sonia.

'I wonder what Stella will say…'

'I'm sure she'll be thrilled,' Sonia replied.

The old lady muttered something and fiddled in her handbag. Then the funeral entourage appeared and filed down to the front. They lay the coffin on a splint and the undertakers retired to the shadowed recess of the church.

Sonia craned her neck piecing together the family. Stella sat beside Jenny and Trevor with the two boys. Freddie is married to Hannah and they had three children who were too young to be at the funeral. Iain sat beside a tall slim blond woman with thin lips, and it was Mark in his crumpled suit who seemed to be alone.

Sonia followed the service. She prayed, she sang and when it came to the eulogy she learned about their lives and family anecdotes; where they lived and what Milton liked and the type of man he was and of their frequent trips to the family beach hut on warm summer evenings. Milton was devoted to Stella and he adored his five grandchildren.

They were the perfect family.

At the end of the service the vicar remind the congregation that Milton and the family would like to invite them to the Hotel for some light refreshments.

The procession left. Sonia had a view of them all. Stella clutching a wad of damp tissues hung on Jenny's arm. The men followed stoically behind with the tall blond woman and the children, and as he passed by her pew, Mark's eyes rested again on Sonia.

'Are you coming to the Hotel?' she asked the old lady and when she nodded Sonia linked her arm through hers. 'We can go together, if you like.'

Sonia noticed the elegance. The triangle-cut sandwiches, tea served in bone china cups and steaming rich coffee were all laid out and waiting on a pristine linen tablecloth before a roaring fire. As far as funerals went, this was one of the best that Sonia had attended. She tasted an egg and cress sandwich and then ate a piece of chocolate cake.

'He didn't want people wearing black,' Sonia said, when the old lady introduced her to a group of retired teachers.

'You look very pretty, dear,' another replied.

'Do you know the family well?' asked another.

'I did – a long time ago – we were just children. My mother knew them much better-'

'Did you live in Chestfield?'

'We moved, let me see, that must have been…oh, thank you. These sandwiches are delicious. Have you tried the egg and cress? I remember growing cress with Iain or was it Freddie? I can't remember, I do muddle them up.'

'Do you? But they are all so different.'

Sonia felt the gaze of her small group on her and she laughed. 'They weren't when they were younger…'

'Ah, here comes, Mark.' The foppish man in the group

with a red bowtie waved him over. 'I think he's going to join us.'

Sonia's heart skipped and she concentrated on the trembling china tea-cup in her hand.

Mark smiled. 'Dad would have been thrilled to see so many people here today. This is a real celebration of his life.'

'It was so sudden,' says one.

'Such a shock.'

'How's Stella coping? They were inseparable,' asks the old lady.

Mark sighed and shrugged. 'It won't be easy.'

His eyes rest on Sonia and he is about to speak to her when the old lady tugged on his arm.

'And where have you been?'

'On a dig – in the Artic.'

'Find anything?' asked Mr Foppy bowtie.

'Skeletal remains, I think, we'll know next week when I get-'

'Your father would be so proud,' the old lady interrupted.

Then to Sonia's dismay Mark is caught up in greeting someone else and is whisked away. She uses this opportunity to freshen up in the Ladies and she is applying lipstick when Jenny walks in. Their eyes meet in the mirror and they smile sadly.

'Have we met?' Jenny asks.

Sonia pushes the lipstick into her bag and zips it firmly closed.

'I'm Sonia – we had a beach hut near yours.'

'Really? I don't remember?'

'My father used to talk to Milton…on the beach.'

'Really? Did we play together?'

'I was a little younger, no-one had time for me,' Sonia laughs.

'Any brothers or sisters?'

'No.'

'I wondered if Freddie, Iain or Mark might have played with-'

'I did speak to the boys a few times when I was with my father but they wouldn't remember it was a long time ago.'

'And then you came here ...today...how kind.'

'Well, my Dad and Milton still saw each other – up until the end.'

'They did?'

'Yes.'

'Is your father with you?'

'No, he, er, he passed away suddenly...'

'I'm sorry. But it's nice of you to come.'

'Well, don't let me stop you...' Sonia nods at the cubicle and smiles. She has just reached the door when Jenny calls out.

'How long ago did your father pass away?'

'Only a few months ago.' Sonia dips her head at the door and disappears. She hangs onto the stair rail conscious of the stares of those below looking up at her and decides on one last cup of tea.

'We haven't met,' Mark says coming to stand beside her near the window. 'Would you like to speak to Mum?'

Sonia is unable to resist him as he takes her elbow and guides her to the grieving widow.

Sonia takes Stella's hand in hers. 'I'm sorry for your loss.'

'Thank you. How... how did you know Milton?'

'I didn't know him well at all. My father and he… were close.'

'Really?' Stella looked surprised. 'Who was your father?'

'Matthew Brooks. He was an historian. I think they consulted on history things… and they chatted about everything.' Sonia sipped her tea and watched Jenny descend the stairs.

'I don't remember the name,' Stella said. 'Does your father still work? Milton was retired.'

'Yes – Dad was too. I think they chatted on the phone a lot.'

'Really?' Stella frowned at Mark.

Mark smiled. 'I think I remember.'

'Really? You do?' said Sonia. 'We had a beach hut.'

'Yes. Of course,' Mark smiled.

When Sonia smiled she looks attractive. Not at all fat and jolly like they say she looked, in the chip shop, where she works most evenings.

As Jenny joined them Sonia is forgotten and she slips away unnoticed. She walked to the town centre and on the bus she kicked off her shoes. Her feet are sore and her ankles are swollen. She tapped the seat with a purple nail thinking about the events of the past few hours.

It had all gone very well. She sighed and pulled the newspaper from her bag and scanned the obituary page.

Would she have time for another funeral this week?

Mark had potential. He was the only single and eligible one there but he was going back to the Arctic and Sonia wasn't hanging around. Her clock was ticking too quickly. There must be another funeral she could go to on her day off.

She'd met some lovely people today and had a wonderful time. It certainly beats sitting at home alone or conversing in a chat room.

She didn't know why more people hadn't thought of doing it.

It was much more fun than a dating website and far more exciting.

All Inclusive

'It's ridiculous to fly all this way to the Caribbean and not see anything…' He didn't turn around and I could barely hear him. His voice drifted away, right over the hotel's tropical gardens; colourful flowers, exotic bushes and lush palm trees with fronds that looked as though they'd been polished for our arrival. His irritable words seemed to float away and disappear into the Atlantic and I just caught the tail end of his sentence. 'I thought this place would be more, you know, accessible and we could go out-'

'But you knew it was all inclusive-'

'Yes, but not that it was in the middle of nowhere.'

'You saw the website.' I kept my voice deliberately calm and pulled my towel over my breasts, relishing the soft sweet aroma of the body milk I'd rubbed in after my shower. It was expensive and I'd bought it especially for this holiday.

'Even the taxi driver said we had to be careful if we left the resort. Well, it's not even a resort, is it? It's a mini village. It's like two weeks of living in Clacton but with heat and mosquitoes-'

'You said you were tired and you wanted to sunbathe and read and do nothing. Now it seems you want to go sightseeing. Have we come on the wrong holiday, James?'

'Christ, now look! There's even a wedding down there on the beach, look! How crass is that?'

'It's romantic,' I say standing beside him. My neck and shoulders aching down to my waist and I yawn. My body is still jet-lagged and I lift my chin to rest on his shoulder. Below us hotel staff are preparing a secluded area on the beach; laying out three neat rows of four chairs with white covers and blue bows. Two young boys erect an archway and secure it in the white powder sand and a waitress appears carrying fresh red and yellow flowers that she weaves between the latticed frame-work of the arch.

'Romantic?' He squints at the scene below and turns away. 'It's tacky. I'd hate it.'

'Why?' I try to hide the disappointment in my voice and realise I'm not altogether successful. He stands with his back to the scene contemplating the terrace table littered with magazines, old newspapers and books from our flight.

I focus on a small group gathering in the garden. 'That's the bride or groom's family arriving I suspect,' I whisper as a small group begin to take their seats.

'It's not normal, is it? It's too posy - too, *oh look at us, we're in love and we got married in the Caribbean,*' he says in a falsetto voice and although I laugh at his imitation of a newly wedded bride, I'm also irked.

'Cynic.'

'Come on, Frances, you'd hate it too.' He reaches for my hand but I avoid his grasp and shake him off. My towel comes loose and I hold it across my breasts.

'Are you going to moan about something all holiday or will we relax and have fun?' I ask. Last night had been amazing. I thought he'd be tired and want to sleep. We'd both been a little drunk from our flight but he'd been flirty and then after dinner, relentless and powerful. In truth, I was still a little sore.

'What do you mean? We are having fun, aren't we? What more do you want? Sex on the Beach?' His mouth turns into a naughty smile.

'Talking of which, let's go down to the bar for a cocktail and watch the wedding?'

'I'm sure they water the drinks down. They couldn't possibly use proper rum - a decent brand. It's probably made locally, we saw enough sugar cane growing in the fields. I'm sure that's why my head hurt this morning. It's inferior stuff and they dilute it with-'

'You seemed to like it enough last night,' I smile.

'We'd just arrived and I was thirsty.' He looks back down over the balcony. 'Oh god, would you really want to get married abroad? Christ, please tell me you wouldn't Frances…'

'I can think of worse places to get married than here. Look James, it's idyllic: palm trees, sunshine, a beautiful beach and colourful gardens. What's not to like?'

'You'd probably want your family here too, wouldn't you?'

'Are you proposing James?'

'No, I'm just saying. It's not for everyone. It wouldn't be right for us, you know, if we decided one day that we might want to get married…'

'I think some of my family would fly over. We could

combine it with a holiday, like they've done.' My gaze rests on the group below. A chubby man is sweating heavily in a white suit and he wipes his forehead with a handkerchief. He's smiling at someone who's hidden behind a group of palm trees and he's bantering with another man who looks like his best man. 'He seems happy, James. It's a big day for them - it's forever.'

'Well, I wouldn't wear a white suit,' James mumbles. He turns away and picks up a discarded IT magazine.

'White would suit you, so to speak,' I smile and leaning over his shoulder I kiss his cheek. 'You'd look very handsome.'

'I might but look at that, all those people sitting on the beach, half-naked watching it all. It's like a live *Big Brother* programme. You'd feel a right idiot performing in front of them all.'

'They're not naked. They've got swimwear on. Besides, what's to perform? You're not a film star. You're getting married. And if you were in love, like that man down there, you wouldn't care what anyone else says or thinks. It's about you and your bride - the woman you marry - the woman you love.'

'But they'd all be watching, staring and-'

'Criticising?'

'Exactly.'

'No more than they did last night when you spun me around too quickly on the dance floor.'

'No-one noticed.'

'What? That you let go and I was flung across the floor?'

'My hand slipped.'

'I thought you were going to say it was that cheap rum,

the one that you had so much of, but instead it was your sweaty palm.'

'So, you are still angry?'

'No, but I'm sure people were watching us last night and probably thought you were drunk. People have a funny way of seeing things differently. Like you now, with them.'

I turn my attention away from him and lean over the balcony. The groom and his best man have been joined by several other guests. 'Shall we go down and watch from the bar?' I suggest.

'Watch the wedding?'

'Why not. Come on, the sun will be going down soon and we can look at the sunset. It will be beautiful - and romantic.'

James clears his throat and focuses on the magazine in his hand.

'Well, we don't have to if you don't want to. We can stay here and just go down for dinner later.' I sit down, cross my legs and pick up my book deliberately ignoring James but I'm curious and I take surreptitious glances through the balcony glass. A woman that I assume is the bride's mother appears wearing a floppy white sunhat that covers most of her face.

James looks at me. 'Are you upset, Frances?'

'No.'

'Really?'

'I promise. I told you when we started going out together that I have no expectations. I just want to hang out and have fun.'

'I know but-'

'I'm not like Claire. I'm not anything like your ex.

We're the complete opposite, James. I'm me. I'm very relaxed and laid back. I have no urgency to have a ring on my finger or to get married. Although, if or when it does happen - then I shall be happy because I won't do it until I know I've met the right man.'

'Aren't I the right man?'

'I haven't decided.'

He leans down and kisses my lips. 'I'm sorry I'm sometimes grouchy. How quickly can you be dressed? We might make it down there before the bride appears.'

Ten minutes later my high heels clip on the tiles as we cross the bar and I climb up onto the bar stool. From my vantage point I can see the wedding guest. The groom's family have the same round faces, pink cheeks and smiling brown eyes.

James leans on the bar and orders champagne.

'Really?' I ask taking a glass of the sparkling liquid.

'We're on holiday. We have to celebrate, Frances.' His amber eyes twinkle and he places his arm across my shoulder and we clink glasses. 'I'm sorry, it's not us.' He kisses my cheek.

'Are you, really?'

He laughs. 'No. I'm a more traditional kind of guy. Local village church, that sort of thing-'

'Is that what you planned before Claire left?'

'Kind of-'

Music suddenly comes out of the speakers. It's louder than it should be and we grimace. The barman calls out and someone turns down the theme tune to *Titanic* but Celine Dion's strong voice gusts dramatically around us like a simmering storm.

'That's not a good sign, ' I say.

'What?'

'It's doomed,' I giggle.

'I like this song.'

'Really, James? I didn't think you like that type of slush. Bet you hated the film?'

'No. I actually liked it. It was-' he pauses and when I look at him he isn't looking at me but his eyes are focused on the optics behind the bar.

'You're missing the wedding. Turn around. The woman with the floppy hat over her eyes looks like the bride's mother.'

She's standing with a younger woman who has dark hair and almond-shaped eyes - the best friend? They are looking anxious and excited waiting for the bride.

'What do you think she'll wear, James? Do you think she'll have a white wedding dress? Wouldn't it be funny if she wore black? No-one would expect that, would they?'

'This really isn't my thing,' he says leaning on the bar. 'I feel we're intruding.'

'Come on, look! They want us to watch. It's all part of their special day. Look at them!'

James won't turn around. Instead he focuses on the barman and orders more champagne. The bar fills up and hotel guests watch the events unfold. Near the archway, a handsome, ebony faced priest waits in a white, burgundy and purple robe. He clutches a bible to his chest and his teeth shine in greeting.

Sam Smith sings *Stay with Me*. 'I love this song,' I say humming along, keeping rhythm with my toe. I hold out my glass to the barman who refills it for me while James glances at the beach but he turns away leaning on the bar. Beside us an older couple are swaying in time to the music and singing to each other.

'Here comes the bride, wow! Isn't she gorgeous? She's radiant. Now, that's how a bride should look!'

Her short white dress is cut low over her tanned breasts. Her hair is braided like the locals and she carries a posy of white and blue flowers. Her smile seems as wide as the ocean and her excited happiness fills the pit of my stomach with warmth.

'James, watch.' I dig him in the ribs and eventually he turns around. 'She looks so happy. Isn't she gorgeous?' I link my arm through his but his body is tense. 'Let's go to the reception and see if we can book an excursion or something to do tomorrow?' I lean against his shoulder enjoying the strength of his broad muscular frame but I can't take my eyes from the wedding scene.

Her brother, who is giving her away, has the same dark eyes and full lips. Very slowly she turns and looks over her shoulder. She seems to take it all in; the sunset, the beach, the gardens and the bar. It's as if she wants to remember this minute, this occasion, for the rest of her life.

'It's so important,' I sigh and it's like she can hear me and our eyes lock and suddenly she blinks and turns away. Disconcerted I exhale. I hadn't realised I was holding my breath. 'It's very emotional, isn't it, James?' I nudge him. His body is hard and firm from his lunch-time training in the gym. He's rigid like a solid statue and I nudge him.

'James? Where do you want to go tomorrow? How about deep sea fishing, would you like that?'

He doesn't answer.

The bride and her brother walk slowly between the chairs toward the priest and John Legend sings, *All of Me*. I know all the words so I join in, quietly whispering.

The groom stuffs the handkerchief in his pocket and smiles at his future wife. I know it's their wedding but it's a day that I know I will remember - forever.

'This is our song, isn't it, James?'

It had been out for a few months when we started dating. We'd met at an IT conference in London and after a long day of training seminars we'd gone to a pub and got a little drunk and James had sung it to me. He told me about his breakup and we spent hours talking. He never married Claire but she had kept their house and mortgage after they separated. Fortunately they never had children. Never got around to it, he said. Then she'd had an affair with a consultant at the hospital where she worked. I saw myself as his saviour and I stepped in and mended his heart. We dated a few months before I asked him to move in with me and he didn't mention her after that. It had taken almost six months.

I slip my arm contentedly though his and kiss his cheek. 'I'm so pleased we came on holiday, James. We really need this break.'

The groom moves from one foot to the other while his bride appears calm. I wonder what life they will have ahead of them. What fortune will shine upon them - perhaps children? The couple are speaking their parts in clear voices. The priest's words: togetherness, love, tenderness and care are carried on the warm breeze and they wrap themselves around me like a protective aura and I beam happily.

'Would you like a boy or a girl?' I whisper.

James's voice is hoarse. 'A girl.'

'Why? So, that you can walk her up the aisle?' I smile.

'What?'

'You will have to walk our daughter up the aisle when she gets married.'

The bride and groom kiss. There's spontaneous applause and family and friends gather around the newly married couple. James straightens his back. He looks tired. The jet-lag and hangover have caught up with him and he looks sick.

Christina Perri sings *A Thousand Years*.

'Great music choices, don't you think? They're all our favourites.'

James rubs his forehead. 'Let's go. Come on, we'll have an early dinner and go to bed?' He takes my arm and I hop down from the bar stool and dodge the dancing couple but by this detour, our path crosses with the wedding party. They're making their way to a table set with canapés and drinks and we are suddenly caught up in their emotion and laughter. A ripple of excitement travels through me and I think I'm the bride and that this is *my* day and these people are my family. I straighten my hunched shoulders and for the first time in my life I believe I'm slim, tanned, tall and beautiful. Not overweight, pale-skinned and hollow-eyed: too many late nights staring at a computer screen solving IT problems and eating junk food. Then suddenly I'm in front of the beautiful bride: face to face. Her freshness, her happiness and her aura of beauty are overwhelming but as she glides around me her smile fades and her aura of happiness dissipates into the cloudless Caribbean sky and a frown crosses her forehead. She stops. She is about to speak to me and I smile.

'James?' she says.

He stands like a wooden soldier.

'What the f-'

'Claire,' he mumbles.

The groom's chubby smile fades.

'Oh my god!' The bride's mother with the floppy hat exclaims. 'You've got a bloody cheek turning up here.'

The bride's brother pushes past the groom. His fist flies past me and he smacks James in the face.

Blood spurts from his nose. I gasp and cover my mouth.

In the confusion a man says, 'Oh shit, you couldn't make this up.'

All Exclusive

When Pete, my best-man, says, 'Oh shit, you couldn't make this up.' I'm standing like a useless statue. To say I'm bewildered is an understatement. It's my bloody wedding day and just a few minutes ago Claire was radiant and happy, promising to love me forever. Now she's a mass of tears and incoherent words.

Pete pulls Billy away before he can land another punch. He's always been protective of his sister but to thump someone in public like that…

The girl he's with looks as shocked as me but she musters quickly. There's blood flowing down the guy's shirt and she drags him away toward the reception and the lifts without a backward glance.

They disappear but I'm still reeling. I'm about to put my arm around Claire's shoulders but she's looking at her mother in that silent way they often use to communicate. It excludes me so I shove my hands into my pockets.

When she dissolves into tears Barbara pushes me aside and takes charge. She leads Claire away and it's Sheena who mumbles something about them going to the toilet, makeup and hair.

My family fall away taking an agitated Billy with them and when they're gone Pete slaps my shoulder. 'Come on, let's go to the bar and have a drink.'

I can't move. My world has collapsed. I'm locked in my own world. It happens in a crisis. I go rigid and I can't function. That's why I was never a surgeon, or worked in A&E. I'm just a simple doctor.

'You alright, Roger?'

'I don't know what to think, Pete. What just happened? Who the hell was that idiot on our holiday, at our wedding - on our bloody honeymoon?'

'I guess Claire will tell you. She'll explain.' He pulls me beside him and I stumble. I have trouble putting one foot in front of the other.

'Perhaps when she stops crying. She seems pretty cut up...' I turn back unable to tear my gaze away from Claire who's now on the far side of the bar. She's with her mother but she is leaning against Sheena. It's Sheena, her best friend, who is speaking and in control. Claire's eyes are closed.

I sigh.

'Let's get a drink and leave them to sort it.' Pete grabs my elbow.

Periodically Sheena glances over at us but she doesn't wave and for the first time since we met, I don't resent her being with Claire.

'I feel a complete idiot and on top of everything, I'm too bloody hot.' I slip off the white jacket that Claire insisted I wear and place it over the bar stool. It had been a good idea last May, standing in Debenhams with the air conditioning on but now I am sweltering.

We sit on stools and I feel the inquisitive gaze of the guests around me, the adoring fans who had watched us wed a few minutes ago on the beach have now been witness to this unsightly brawl.

The older couple beside us give me a sympathetic smile. They were dancing a few minutes ago and I want to shout and tell them to bugger off but I don't. I close my eyes and rub my head while Pete orders beer for us both.

'What are they doing?' I don't want to turn around.

'They've gone.'

'Gone?'

'Yup.'

'For christsake, Pete. Where to?'

He shrugs. 'The bathroom?'

'What about our lot?'

'They've gone to our table.'

'Do you think I should do something?'

'Nah. They're fine. They've got drinks. Let it all settle down and see what happens.'

We sink our beer very quickly and when there's still no sign of Claire, Pete orders another.

'Someone will have to appear soon,' I say. 'Dinner is booked at eight. Who was that bloke, do you know him?' I'd been bottling up the question but now I had to ask. Pete's a decent guy. He'd give me the heads up on anything. He's a straight-talker and even if the news was bad he'd tell you anyway. He has what patients call a good bedside manner. 'Never seen him at the hospital, have you?'

Pete shakes his head. 'I don't think he's from the hospital.'

'What did she say, exactly, do you remember what Claire said?'

'I couldn't hear very well.'

'Billy must know who he is, where's he gone?'

Pete shrugs.

'Maybe they're getting a story together.'

I wipe my forehead with my handkerchief, pleased that the sun has finally set. Even in the evening it's still too humid for me and I sigh as the evening lights are switched on. The swimming pool changes from deep red to lilac and the garden shrubs seem wax-like and glisten under the lamplight. Only the invisible crickets are huddled together still shrilling and shrieking as if nothing's happened.

'What do you mean, Roger?'

'Maybe Billy's not allowed near us.'

Pete pats my shoulder. 'Do you want to go up to your room and find her?'

'I don't know.'

'You can't sit here forever.'

'I guess not but I thought Claire would have come to find me by now. I thought she'd have calmed herself down and come to explain things. Maybe…maybe…'

'Maybe what?'

'Maybe even apologised… Perhaps she's not who I thought she was.'

'I'm sure she is. It will all be fine. Things have a funny way of working out. You'll see.' Pete smiles but his bedside manner doesn't work on me. Not this time.

'Do you think he was her ex?' I call out to the barman. 'Give me a whiskey chaser.'

'Is that a good idea?' Pete frowns.

'It's the only one I've got.' I swivel around on my seat and lean my back against the bar. In the past hour the seats and the wedding arch have been removed from the beach. Even the priest has been swallowed up. There's no sign of our wedding. No sign that it was a special day. Even the other hotel guests have lost interest in me and have drifted off to one of the five restaurants on the complex.

'Bloody hell, if it is her ex, just think… of all the places to bump into them,' I groan. 'Do you think he knew she was here and we were getting married?'

'Stalking her?' Pete shakes his head. 'I think it's a strange coincidence.'

'Do you think she still loves him?'

'Don't be crazy. She loves you, Roger that's why she married you.'

'Then where is she?'

'Do you want to go up to the room?'

'I suppose I'll have to.' I slide off the stool and Pete walks with me through the tropical gardens, past the Italian themed restaurant where the smell of garlic bread fills my nostrils. 'What about the table for dinner?' I ask.

'I'll sort it. You go and speak to Claire. I'll look after the rest of the guests.'

He waits with me until the lift arrives.

'Thanks mate,' I whisper and he pulls me into a bear hug. He slaps my back and pushes me away and into the lift.

'Just remember how much you love her,' he says as the lift door closes. When it opens again I walk sluggishly along the corridor and hesitate outside the door with my key in my hand.

I knock. I wait.

Sheena opens the door. Her almond eyes regard me without emotion and instant loathing springs into my mind but I keep my expression neutral. There's only so much I can take - especially on such an important day.

'Is Claire here?'

'Yes.' She doesn't open the door so I step inside and push past her.

'Claire?' I call out.

She's laying across our king-sized bed and when she sees me she attempts to sit up. Screwed up tissues are tossed on the floor and across the duvet. Her shoes that we bought the same day as my white suit are strewn under the bed. We laughed that day only a few months ago, excited at our wedding plans, and now it's all a fiasco.

'I want to be alone with my wife,' I say over my shoulder to Sheena who stands watching us.

'Will you be okay?' She asks my wife and Claire nods.

Sheena picks up her handbag and on her way out she shouts. 'Call me if you need me.'

I wait but Claire doesn't speak. I feel anger rising inside me and to stop it from welling up and exploding, I sit down in the chair by the window. I grip my fingers into fists blocking out the memory of our love-making with her on my lap just a few days ago on this seat.

'I think I deserve an explanation, don't you?'

Her eyes are swollen and bloodshot. Her nose is red and bulbous and she looks so forlorn I want to reach out and hold her. But I can't. I can't move. I don't trust myself.

She reaches for another tissue.

'Why are you crying, Claire?'

'Because, because….'

'Are you pleased you married me?'

She frowns and looks at me from under her fringe. The beads on her long hair clinking together as she swings her head. 'Of course.'

'It doesn't appear that way.'

'I'm upset-'

'So am I.'

'It was a shock-'

'Who is he?'

'I knew him a while ago…before-'

'You went out together?'

'We shared a house.'

'You lived with him?'

'Yes.'

'And you didn't tell me?'

'It was in the past.'

'But you could still have told me. What's his name.'

'James.'

'Is he a doctor?'

'Does it matter?'

'I suppose not. How did he know we were getting married?'

She shrugs. 'I don't know. It must be a coincidence.'

'That only happens in bad films. This resort is massive. It has five restaurants, twelve tennis courts and a gym so why did he happen to end up at our wedding, unless he knew about it?'

'I've no idea.'

'Are you telling me the truth?'

Her teary eyes stare back at me. 'Of course I am.'

'Okay, so assuming it's a coincidence, you'd better tell

me who he is.'

She reaches for another tissue, swings her legs around on the bed and props up her head with the pillows against the headboard. 'His name is James. We went out for a few years.'

'When was it over?'

'Last year.'

'Before we started dating?'

'Yes.'

'So, why did you never mention him?'

'He wasn't important.'

'Well, he clearly was today. For Chrissake, Billy punched him. Why?' I stand up and pace to the bathroom door before opening the door to the minibar. I select a whiskey, unscrew the cap and drink from the miniature bottle, concentrating on my burning throat.

'He hurt me.' Her voice is low and husky.

'How?' I sit beside on the bed but we don't touch.

'We were going to get married but then he left.'

'Why?'

'I don't know.'

'You must.'

'No, I really don't. I just came home one day from my shift and there was a note and his clothes were gone.' She dabs her eyes.

'What did it say?'

'I don't remember, something like: *I'm not for you. You'll be better off without me. I won't be in touch ever again...*'

'But he never said why?'

'No.'

'So who was the girl with him?'

Claire shrugs. 'I've never seen her before. It must be his

new girlfriend.'

I study Claire's face. Although I'd seen her around the hospital and in the canteen we'd never actually spoken until a year ago. When I asked her to marry she agreed immediately. I couldn't believe a girl like her would fall for a bloke like me. So I decided to do it right away. We'd booked our holiday to include the wedding and the honeymoon on the same day we bought my suit and Claire's shoes. We never dreamed some of our family and friends would join us and it was a small, perfect, wedding party. Only Claire's dad hadn't been able to come. He lived and worked in France but she hadn't been bothered and I said I'd take her to Paris later in the year, so she could show him her wedding ring.

I trace the red line in the Aztec design of the duvet trying not to touch her leg and run my hand up the inside of her thighs as I did last night.

Was she telling me the truth?

It hardly seems possible that we'd made love last night. We said we wouldn't on the eve of our wedding. We'd even considered separate rooms but then we hadn't been able to help ourselves. I found it hard at the best of times not to touch her and we'd giggled and pretended we were on our stag and hen do, having one final fling. I'd felt so lucky to think she'd marry a guy like me; overweight and balding and I couldn't quite believe it. Now, my bubble had burst and there was a gaping hole in my heart.

'What do you want to do?' she asks.

'Me?'

'Yes, do you still want me?'

'Of course I do.'

She leans forward and a fresh spill of tears well up in

her eyes so I pull her into my arms, kissing her forehead. I kiss her wet cheeks and mumble her name. 'I just need to know one thing,' I whisper.

'What?' her voice is breathless.

'Do you still love him?'

'No, silly. Of course I don't. I love you.'

'Promise?'

'Pinky promise.' We link little fingers, as we have done since we met, and a ripple of warmth surges through my veins and I smile.

'That's all I need to know.' I squeeze her tightly reassured by her kiss and the probing tip of her tongue and then I pull away. 'Come on Mrs Westward. Let's go and celebrate. Our guests are waiting downstairs.'

'But what about-'

'Who?'

'Them. What will they say?'

'There's nothing to worry about. It's our business. Come on, I'm bloody starving.'

All Encompassing

'Come on, Sheena. One last one?' Pete picks up the wine bottle and deliberately brushes against my breasts. 'I didn't have you down as a party pooper.'

I know what doctors are like; all professional and businesslike during the day but as soon as they party they turn into leering and lecherous werewolves, and try to bed everything in sight.

I've a headache and I want to go home. I want to be back in London. The tension in my shoulders and neck is making my head thump and I want to go to bed but true to form Pete is playing the dutiful part of the best man. Recently divorced, he's now trying to flirt with me. It's the old scenario of best man and bridesmaid but I'm not interested. There are enough dirty secrets around this table and I don't need any more.

I've picked at my food barely able to eat. Periodically I glance around the table. Barbara is holding court at the far end. She's very attractive, well-groomed, well-dressed and well-spoken. She sits beside Roger's gay aunt and her partner and they're all pretty sloshed. As yet no-one is inclined to leave the dinner table and I wonder if it's because they're frightened the fragility of the gaiety will disappear.

'What did you have me down for?' I ask but I don't look at Pete. My gaze is now on Claire and Roger, on the far side of the table, intermittently kissing and laughing. Whatever she told him in the bedroom he must have believed. He looks happy again and even she looks relieved.

She won't meet my eyes. Deliberately. She can't. It's our secret. We know that Roger is jealous of our friendship and we play it down when he's around. I know she has to make him feel special, especially after today, after that awful scene.

Barbara doesn't look at me either. She's another one who is jealous. She always said I was a bad influence on Claire but it's not true. I'm her best mate. Closer than her mother, her brother Billy and even closer than her own husband. No one could guess the level of my faithfulness and my determination to keep Claire happy.

'I know that surgeon broke your heart. And if it's any consolation, he's an idiot and I always thought you were pretty hot.' Pete's sweet alcoholic breath is near my face.

'Even for a radiologist?'

He laughs. 'Yup but you're too aloof. I don't know. Uptight. You have to lighten up. Do you have sex?'

'Most nights,' I laugh.

'On your own?' He places his hand on my knee and laughs.

'Don't knock it till you've tried it,' I smile.

'I'd like to try it with you.' He puts his other arm

around the back of my chair.

Barbara looks up. She's watching us. So is Claire and so is Roger. But I don't care. I've done it. I saved their marriage so I might as well have a little fun with Pete besides, half of the nurses in the hospital said he was good in bed.

'I'm not your type,' I whisper.

'Yes you are,' he laughs. His hand moves up my bare skin. 'You're very much my type and I love your legs.'

'They're short and dumpy.'

'They would fit around me,' he whispers. The hairs inside my ear quiver from his hot breath and a shiver of excitement ripples through my body.

'Nah,' I say and reach for my wine glass.

'You're a dark horse,' he says. 'I bet you know more than you're letting on.'

'About what?'

He lowers his voice. 'Who was that bloke in the bar this afternoon. Is Claire still in love with him.'

I pull away and look aghast. 'Don't be crazy. Can't you see she only has eyes for Roger.'

His hand travels slowly up the inside of my leg. 'I bet you know who he is. Want to tell me?'

'It's none of my business. It's for them to sort out.'

He laughs and kisses my cheek. I'm surprised his lips are so soft. 'I think, you know a lot more than you're letting on-'

'It's not for me to speak about their relationship.'

He takes the lobe of my ear between his lips and I shudder and lean closer to him. Nerves tingle in my body and a wave of excitement sends goose pimples along my skin.

When I open my eyes Barbara is staring at me. She's taken off that ridiculous floppy hat she's worn all day and now she's flirting with Roger's aunt but I know she's watching me like a cat. The Hooded Claw I call her when Claire and I are alone.

'The what?' Pete says laughing. 'Hooded Claw? Is that a sex toy.'

'Could be,' I murmur.

His index finger is under my skirt sliding closer to my thong.

'Are we going clubbing?' Billy leans across the table. Although the plates, food and debris have been cleared it's strewn with dirty, empty glasses. 'Who's coming to the disco?' he sings.

'Meeee!' I jump to my feet.

Pete pulls away and looking surprised. 'I thought we were-'

'Later. Come on, let's go.' I pull on his hand and follow Billy and Roger's relatives from the restaurant but near the bar Pete pulls me back and I collapse into his arms, slightly worse for wear and I feel his erection against me.

'Can you be sure he won't be there?'

'Who?' But I know who he means and I link my arm through his. 'Come on Pete, forget about him. He's history.'

We clatter down to the nightclub on the floor below the reception where the music is loud and it's dark. I want to dance with Claire. We love this Rhianna song. She's sticking close to Roger but she gives me a sly wink and then sticks out the tip of her tongue to me and I laugh.

Roger's lesbian aunt and her girlfriend are rocking it on the dance floor and I'm mesmerised watching them;

whooping it up and clapping.

'It's an age thing,' Roger shouts above the music, dragging Claire onto the floor. 'They'll be dying and hungover tomorrow.'

Most of Roger's relatives join the throng on the floor, jiving and dancing and Billy drifts away to another group of people I recognise that he met earlier in the week.

Pete follows him. I know Billy doesn't like Pete and suddenly there's only Barbara left. She's standing beside me waving to the barman who spots her immediately. She has that aura, that charm, that magnetism that angers me - and Claire. But I'm happy when she orders for us both. Leaning across the counter, the barman smiles, his eyes drawn to her brown breasts and deep cleavage. She hasn't changed and she never will. Claire and I grew up together. I know all about her failed marriage and her boyfriends. But I can be trusted with a secret.

She knows that.

When the gin and tonics arrive she clinks my glass against hers.

'It seems like I owe you,' she says.'

'It's about Claire's happiness - not ours.'

'Does Roger know about James?'

'He doesn't have a clue.'

'What did Claire tell him?'

I shrug. 'It's all in the past. Isn't it?'

'Yes.'

'Claire needs to move on.'

'She does.'

'She's happy with Roger. She's safe. No-one will want to sleep with him.' I sip my drink. 'Will they?'

'I shouldn't imagine so.' Barbara is watching her

daughter and new husband slow dancing.

'She'll be safe,' I say.

'She looks happy.'

'That's how I intend to keep her.'

Barbara stares at me and I look away.

Pete is standing with Billy's crowd with a drink in one hand and his arm around a young girl's waist.

'No wonder his wife divorced him,' Barbara says. 'Slime-ball.'

The ice cubes rattle in my glass as I drink. It's probably the only thing Barbara and I will ever agree on and suddenly I feel tired and a little drunk. It's been an emotional day with an unexpected twist.

James.

After the scene played out I couldn't let it go. I'd caught up with James just outside their bedroom door. Blood was still streaming down his face, dripping though his fingers and splashing onto his white shirt. How could I ever have thought he was good looking? He looked defeated and wretched and I felt no compassion toward him but I did feel very sorry for the girl standing beside him. She looked like she actually cared. She wasn't his normal type. This one was heavily built and she tried to stand between me and James, as if she wanted to protect him and I had laughed bitterly.

'He can look after himself. He's always managed that very nicely, haven't you, James?' He hadn't replied so I'd continued baiting him. 'Have you followed her? Stalking her to the altar?'

'No!' It wasn't his denial. He didn't look at me. It was his girlfriend speaking. 'James didn't know. I booked the holiday,' she explained.

'Really?' I want to believe her but I'm familiar with his lies and his manipulation technique.

'It's true,' his voice is strained. 'Frances isn't lying.'

'Is she your girlfriend?'

He doesn't reply but she does. 'We live together.' She puffs out her chest and it makes her look ridiculous. Her pink and white dress is so tight it barely covers her bum and sunburnt legs.

'I thought you'd have learnt your lesson with women, James.'

'Lesson?' Frances says. 'What lesson?'

'Didn't you tell her about Claire?' I ask him.

He shakes his head. His amber eyes plead with me and I realise the power I have at this moment. I know I can destroy their relationship as I did with him and Claire. I know I can tell the truth and not even feel guilty. Why should a snake like James get away with it? But I stay silent. I keep my lips sealed only because of the hope in Frances's eyes and the fact that she reminds me of Roger. They're not that different. Both of them are overweight and nondescript and they have the same bewildered expression. It's as if they can't believe they have caught a beauty: that they're dating a gorgeous person. It's always been their dream and would have remained a dream - had the ideal couple stayed together.

It's only then that I feel a sense of justice. There's a price to pay for being a beautiful person. People like Barbara, Claire and James will always be sexy, attractive and make heads turn. People will always want them.

Now I look at Barbara sipping gin beside me and I feel the intense heat of predatory eyes watching her as she moves provocatively to the music, swaying her hips, gyrating and moving her shoulders.

Men with their partners are glancing furtively at her body, appreciating her rhythm and I wonder what they are thinking: Does she move like this in bed? Does she like sex? Is she up for it?

In my drunken hazy state I want to shout:

YES.

She's a SLUT.

Barbara is smiling at a guy across the bar but she leans over and says to me. 'You need to get laid.' She slides her arm affectionately around my shoulder and her warm spittle trickles against my cheek when she slurs. 'It's a waste you standing here with me. You should be up on the dance floor with the lesbians.'

'At least I didn't sleep with Claire's boyfriend.'

She recoils as if I've slapped her. Her cold and hard eyes narrow and she bites her curled lip.

It was by chance I had popped into Claire's house that night. Not realising her shift had changed and I found out James and Barbara were having regular sex. I caught them. I couldn't hide my disgust and in payment for my silence James wrote the note. I watched him pack and he left immediately.

Barbara had pleaded with him to stay with her but James and I knew it wasn't an option.

I had to protect Claire. She is like my own sister. Barbara may hate me but she is lucky. Even though she doesn't deserve it she still has her daughter's love.

I know Claire would never have forgiven her mother.

Dating For A Dad

I type slowly. My fingers carefully stabbing at the keyboard. I hesitate briefly before reading it again.

Personal profile:

I enter Helen Bennett: dark blond hair, green eyes and very attractive.

Characteristics: widow, two children, accountant, non-smoker and occasional drinker.

'What are you doing Jake?' says Anastasia, my seven-year old sister.

'Could you get that Barbie out of my way?' I push the doll away from the screen. I'm four years older and way too grown-up for her stupid toys.

Describe yourself: honest, reliable and kind.

Anastasia's sweet breath is warm against my cheek as she leans forward to inspect the screen.

'Who's that?' She points at a face - one of the dating profiles - a man with a beard. I scroll quickly through the hopefuls that are registered on the site to find a perfect partner.

There seem to be hundreds of them.

'Jake, tell me,' Anastasia whines, twisting her small body onto the seat beside me.

I ignore her.

What type of relationship are you looking for?

I shake my head. This was more complicated than I thought. I can't write friendship, serious or marriage so I settle for what others have written: casual.

'I'm finding you a Daddy,' I whisper, flicking through photographs posted on the site. 'But we mustn't tell Mummy, it's a secret - a surprise.'

Anastasia is balanced precariously on the stool beside my bed. Her right hand clutches her Barbie and the fingers on her left hand twist the fine strands of her long blond hair. Her blue eyes shine in delight.

'A real Daddy?' she repeats. 'A Daddy for us?'

I read quickly. For a bit extra I can upgrade to premier membership then I can email at least six of the men listed in our local area. I have fifty pounds saved in my bank so I'll pay her back. I'm not a thief. I've only *borrowed* her credit card and I've already replaced it in her handbag.

What is she looking for? I type in: He must have a good sense of humour and be intelligent and kind. Then I add, he must love children and football.

'Just don't mention it to Mum. It's our secret.' I smile and close my iPad just as the bedroom door opens.

'What's going on, Jake? I've been calling you both for ages.' Mum frowns suspiciously and then her gaze rests on Anastasia. She's always a soft touch for the truth.

'Nothing,' I say.

I know that look. The way Mum tilts her head to one side and half frowns, although her eyes are smiling. I know she wants more information and she's very clever at reading me and Anastasia. Sometimes I see that same look on Anastasia's face when she is quizzing me. I try not to squirm or fidget.

'Bedtime,' Mum announces. Anastasia scrambles quickly from the chair and, with Barbie tucked under her arm, scuttles from my bedroom.

I'm saved so I sigh and flop back onto the bed.

I listen to them in the bathroom. All the comforting night-time routines; clean teeth, clean hands and face. Running feet along the landing, pyjamas, a story and then kisses goodnight.

I follow that same routine but on my own but I have long since given up the cuddling stuff. I *am* eleven and I've just started senior school. Only occasionally do I throw my arms around Mum and that's when I think she looks sad or lonely and I tell her she's the best mum and the nicest mum in the whole world. She often sighs and that's when she snucks her nose into my neck and smells my skin. It tickles me and always make us laugh. Sometimes she hugs me with such fierce strength like she never wants to let me me go and I worry what she will do when we, Anastasia and I, leave home when we go to University.

'What's dating?' asks Anastasia the next night as she lies sprawled beside me contemplating the photographs I'm swiping on my iPad.

'Kind of like finding the right person to live with.'

'To find a Daddy?'

'Sort of but Mum must like him first before he can be our Daddy. If we can find him for her it will be a nice surprise,' I explain.

'I like surprises,' said Anastasia.

I run my eyes over the answers to my emails. Eric wants to know the ages of my children. He's divorced twice and has six children. William is addicted to fast foods and judging by his photograph he isn't telling any fibs in that department. Trevor hates football and asks if it would be a problem, and Bruce likes rock music and motorbikes which I think would be cool but I know Mum. She likes the comfort of her Audi that comes with her job and classical music. Two guys haven't responded to my email so I am down to four guys that live in our area.

Anastasia looks over my shoulder. 'You said he's going to be my Daddy so that means I can choose too.' She's tired and irritable. 'It's not fair you doing everything, Jake. I want to help with Mummy's surprise. Why can't I choose?'

'Shush, keep your voice down. Okay, alright! So out of these four, who do you like the look of best?' I swipe the photographs on the screen of William, Eric, Trevor and Bruce.

'Ugh, he's ugly,' she says, swiping Bruce aside. 'And this one has a big nose.' She points at Eric. 'And he's got no hair.' Anastasia stabs William's face with her Barbie doll. 'What about him? He's got brown eyes like yours Jake, like in the photos Mummy shows us of Daddy. Do you think he likes Barbies?'

I stare at Trevor's face and shrug. 'He hates football.'

'So do I. Anyway, I like him and so does Barbie!'

'Well that's settled then. That decision's made.' My sarcasm is lost on her but an idea was forming in my head and I suddenly knew what to do - I would test them all - it was easy. We would soon see which of them would still want to meet me or rather meet my mother.

Trevor was the only one who took this change of personality seriously.

In his email he asked why I (my mummy) suddenly liked the idea of sailing and rock climbing? Then he said that if she was willing to try anything then maybe he could too. He said he might even get to like football.

So, maybe Trevor was the one. Divorced, no children and a Financial Director - whatever they did. Besides, Anastasia liked him.

Later that night just before I go to sleep I'm mulling everything over in my head. I lie on my pillow with my hands behind my gelled hair and stare at the ceiling. I don't know if I'm more excited about my first football game on Saturday at my new school or the thought of Mummy meeting someone special.

It had been difficult to describe the type of man she would like to meet. I had tried my hardest to remember all the lovely qualities she said I'd inherited from my father. He died six years ago and although I think I remember him, his memory is sometimes faint. Anastasia whispered to me the other night that she'd almost forgotten him. She remembered him only because of the photographs and videos of us all together. I think we pretend to Mummy that we remember him more than we do because it makes her happy but I have a new plan.

Six years.

Mummy needs a real Daddy for us.

On Saturday I beg Mum, almost dramatically on bended knees, to come to our school football match. It's cold, wet and windy but fortunately she's good-natured and ruffles my hair.

'I'm very proud of you, Jake.'

Later that morning she stands on the sidelines wrapped in her navy and white scarf and warm grey jacket. Beside her Anastasia jumps excitedly up and down. I keep looking up at them. Twice I'm tackled and by half-time there's no sign of Trevor.

The second half is a disaster. I'm worrying that Mummy will be furious when she finds out that I've been on the website and that I used her credit card. If Anastasia starts whinging and whining and says anything about wanting a Daddy then that will be the final straw.

I feel sick.

I miss the ball and fail to score although it's an open goal.

My throat constricts and I spit on the pitch. Glancing at them, Mum and Anastasia continue to shout encouragement but my heart sinks. We're into extra time when a stranger arrives and stands on the touch-line. I recognise him from his photograph and I stop in the middle of the pitch to watch.

Trevor is smiling at Mummy.

They speak and she covers her mouth with her gloved hand, shakes her head and backs away. Trevor digs into his trench coat and pulls out his phone.

Oh no, evidence of our emails.

Mum leans over to look at them and angrily shakes her head. Anastasia reaches up and in her haste she knocks his iPhone to the ground.

As Trevor bends to retrieve it, she points at me.

They all turn.

I barely hear the whistle. I seem to be stuck in the mud. I'm the only one left standing on the torn, wet turf. I can't hear my mother's angry voice. Her words are lost in the wind but I see how she grips Anastasia's hand and holds her close.

Trevor continues talking and occasionally they glance in my direction.

Anastasia breaks away from them and runs toward me shouting.

'You're in big trouble now, Jake. And you're grounded,' she announces breathlessly. 'But he's got a very nice laugh and I think Mummy likes him.'

Trevor stands with his hands in his pockets and he's thrown his head back in laughter but Mum is still frowning. Above us a ray of sunshine escapes from behind the dark, ominous clouds and then Mum's face creases into that peculiar crooked smile and she giggles.

I groan and rub a grubby hand through my hair but they're no longer looking at me. They are both still laughing with each other.

Anastasia smiles up at me, slips her hand into mine and sighs loudly. 'I think we've done it, Jake' she says, squeezing my fingers hard. 'I think I found us a new Daddy.'

They Lied

When did grown ups ever tell the truth?

They lied about Santa, the tooth fairy and the bogeyman.

They said I'd grow tall if I ate my vegetables and they said if I lied that hair would grow on my tongue.

Why believe anyone?

When I met my best friend Chloe at school she said she never wanted children and that men made her sick. We said we'd stay in touch forever but she went off to college and I never saw her again. Last I heard was that she got married and had a baby boy.

George is the owner of the shop where I work. He I should get out more. He said it would do me good and I would meet people and make friends.

'Go to the pub. Go to dancing classes. Join a gym.'

I tried them all.

It didn't work.

I was on my way home form work when I saw a handsome boy at the bus stop. I couldn't look away. His skin was the colour of a rich eggplant blended with a smile as white as a cotton and eyes as green as coriander leaves. His back was rounded like a banana as if the box he was carrying was too heavy for his skinny frame and I wondered what was inside.

While we waited for the bus I took a chocolate bar from my handbag. I peeled away the wrapper and enjoyed the sweet tangy flavours on the side of my tongue, sucking the coco between my teeth and lips.

The bus was packed but I pushed my way to an empty seat at the back. The boy with the box followed me. I sat wedged in at the window but he apologised and I could see from the sadness in his eyes that he was sorry.

'The box is too big to fit on my lap,' he explained, and when another passenger pushed past him the corner dug into his skinny ribs and he let out a surprised gasp.

I looked out of the window and watched the houses stop and start.

The engine rattled up from the floor boards to my toes, through my legs to my stomach and my breasts.

He tried not to look at me but he couldn't help it and I would like to pretend that I was indignant and told him off for staring but I didn't. Instead, I fantasised that he wanted me. I imagined his slim fingers with his ragged nails stroking me, and how my skin would tingle and tickle under his touch.

When two boys across the aisle stared at the package he swung his knees nearer to me and his feet went on on tiptoe. The box swung into my space and rested against my thigh.

He apologised. A lingering curry and garlic aroma from his lips were carried to my tongue and I swallowed thirstily at his exotic airborne spices.

'What's in the box?' The smallest boy across the aisle asked. He stood only a few inches taller than the brown cardboard.

'Don't be nosey.' His mother cautioned tugging on his hand.

'What's in it?' The boy insisted.

'Stop!' The mother turned away to stop her second son from stamping on someone else's foot.

The small boy hit the box with his palm but the boy beside me pulled it protectively to his chest. He leaned forward and in a conspiratorial whisper, he said. 'A dead body.'

I laughed loudly and covered my mouth.

The small boy frowned and pushed his way back between his mother's legs and thumped his brother's shoulder.

The boy beside me grinned and winked so I smiled back.

On the busy street everyone was heading home. It's the end of another tiring day and my feet ached. I heard scratching from inside the box and I turned quickly just as he pulled the box away from my thigh.

The mother and the two boys left the bus at the next stop.

My neighbour ignored them but I watched them from the window and the small boy raised two fingers. It looked like he said the F-word so I stuck out my tongue.

My breasts jangled as the bus swung into the road again.

A line of perspiration formed on the boy's upper lip and he shifted his knees away from me. An old man sat down across the aisle and stared. His spectacles were uneven, unbalanced. They weren't properly on his ears and his wispy hair was combed over his bald plate. He chewed something, not gum, maybe a soft toffee and spoke with his mouthful.

'Looks heavy.' He nodded at the box.

'It is,' Rashid agreed.

'What's in it?'

Rashid hesitated. 'My pet.'

The man tilted his head studying the parcel. 'Have you got air holes?'

Rashid shook his head. 'It's only a short trip.'

'What is it? A hamster?'

'Sort of.'

Their conversation was interrupted as people got on and off but once we're trundling along again the old man persists.

'Gerbil – or rat?'

'Sort of.'

'What? What is it?' The old man asks with the impatience that old people muster when they know they're running out of time and they're in a hurry and don't want to be fobbed off.

'Tell me, it's my stop next.' The old man leaned on his walking stick and grabbed the rail. 'Well?'

'Do you really need to know?" asked Rashid.

'Yes.'

'It's a snake.'

The old man laughed. 'Stupid boy.'

He hobbled down the aisle and as he climbed off the bus he looked back as if he wanted to remember the scene and conversation for the rest of his life – what was left of it.

I thought of the snake inside the box nudging my thigh.

It was gently tapping against me as we rounded the bend, swaying drunkenly against me. The boy went with the rhythm. He had stopped being so protective as the bus become emptier and the last stop became nearer. Although there were empty seats he didn't move away from me. It was as if we had become joined, stuck together in a journey of movement and motion and I wondered what would happen when we got off.

'Excuse me,' I said.

I raised my hand to ding the bell.

His face was at the level of my cleavage. His pointed nose would have fitted perfectly between my breasts but he turned and laid the box on the seat across the aisle, steadied it with his leg and I squeezed past him. It was a tight fit and I brushed against his bottom.

'This is where I get off too,' he said.

I tilted my head.

'Do you want to walk with me – just in case?' he asked.

'In case of what?'

He nodded down at the box. 'It escapes.'

When I jump down from the bus he's behind me. It is already turn to dusk and the yellow street lamps cause dark shadows like giant monsters across the path. I wait until the bus takes off and watch the dim lights fade in the distance.

He tries to smile but the heaviness of the box and the gloominess of the street make him look like the grim reaper.

I turn and walk away from the lights of the shops on the main road and he follows me. He's a few paces behind as I walk toward the residential houses. It becomes darker and the streetlights fade and the only sound are my high heels clipping on the pavement and his laboured breath behind me.

'Do you know where you are?' I ask without turning around.

'I believe so.'

I slow my pace to match his. He's skinny. Half of my width and I'm conscious of my lumbering body beside his graceful gait.

'Are you frightened of snakes?' he asks.

'I don't like them.'

'Why?'

'I don't like the way they slither and slide. I think they also move rather quickly.'

'Does that worry you?'

I don't reply.

'It could kill you.'

'How?'

'It could wrap itself around you and squeeze.'

He struggled with the box to get a better grip as if there was movement inside. He holds his knee in the air and rests before hiking it further in his hands for a better grip. He's skinny but strong.

'If it did that, then I might lose weight – it could squeeze me skinny.'

'You're not fat.'

My heels click until I stop outside the Indian. My favourite restaurant. I inhale the exotic aromas coming from the kitchen vent; turmeric, garam masala and cardamon.

My friend Namdev peers out of the window and

waves. The restaurant is not busy and I can hear the faint twang of the Sitar coming from the old cassette player in the corner.

When Namdev smiles, I wave back.

'Do you eat in here?' he asks.

'I live across the road.' I nod and he follows my eyes to the drab Victorian house now that's converted to flats.

'Can I take your phone number?'

When I don't reply he thrusts the box at me.

'Hold this and I'll write it down.'

I hesitate. Not because I'm not strong enough to hold it. I lug boxes around all day in the Health Shop.

'Here. Take it.' His coriander eyes gleam in the glow from the restaurant but I fold my arms.

'Where are you going now?' I ask. 'I'm going to have dinner if you want to come inside with me.'

He blinks at me. 'This is Indian food?'

'Yes.'

'I'm an Arab.'

'So? Are you hungry? You look like you could do with some feeding up.'

'You won't hold this?' He offers me the box.

'You won't eat with me?' I nod at the restaurant.

A young couple in boots and jeans squeeze past us on the street and as the door to the restaurant opens my stomach rumbles. I can taste the creamy Korma on my tongue and the sharpness of the crisp onion bhajis.

'We will meet again one day,' he says.

It's a lie.

'No, we won't.'

He blinks. 'I have asked for your number.'

'I only meet people who tell the truth and I only want

friends who are honest.'

'Of course.'

'Everyone lies. They lied last week in the paper when they said coffee was bad for you and that red wine should be avoided. This week they say, they're are both good for you and not to eat eggs.'

'They can never decide,' he agrees.

'So what's in the box?'

He hesitates then smiles. 'Gertrude.'

'Who's Gertrude?'

'A writer.'

'The box isn't big enough to hold a dead person.'

'You're wrong.'

'Have you chopped her up?'

'I intend to dissect her mind.'

'Who is she?'

'An archaeologist.'

'Why would you do that?'

'To learn.'

I scratch the pale fleshy mound of my cleavage. 'Is this important to you?'

'She was fluent in Arabic and Persian and she was involved in the reinvention of Mesopotamia…'

'And this means?'

'She was the only woman present at the Cairo Conference with Winston Churchill to determine the boundaries of the Iraqi State and she continues to be studied and referenced by policy experts today.'

'What do you think you will learn?' I ask.

'That the enemy is fear. We think it is hate – but it is fear. Once we conquer this and understand ourselves then we can help other. We can understand others and form lasting world-peace.'

There's a commotion down the street outside the pub. Two men are walking toward us, laughing loudly. One playfully punches the other man's shoulder and the other dummy ducks before throwing a punch at the other man's face. They disappear down an alleyway toward the pub's car park.

'Well,' I say. 'Goodbye and good luck.'

Still holding the package, he shifts his balance and rests it on his forearm. He offers me his hand and wiggles his fingers. There's a gold ring on his baby finger and it twinkles in the streetlight.

I reach out but in that precise moment the restaurant door opens and a woman carrying a plastic carrier bag filled with foil containers hurries down the steps and collides with us.

Food goes up into the air. Flying rice, poppadoms, pickles sauces, Rogan Josh. He falls to the ground and they land on him and he cries out. He drops the box. The lid falls off and it lays open and exposed.

We all lean over the box and a lifeless face stares back at us. Black sockets where the eyes have been and a nose squashed and beaten, now covered in curry sauce.

'Oh no,' he cries.

'What's this?' the woman asks.

'You've spoilt my book.'

He scrambles to his feet and begins wiping the debris from his treasure. A hardback: Gertrude Bell Biography (1868-1926).

'You'll pay for this?' He asks the stranger but she's already gone. She disappears from the mess on the ground and her food at our feet with a stream of angry expletives.

In the glow of the streetlamp a boxful of books was a relief and I begin to laugh.

'Come on. Come and eat something,' I say.

'My name is Rashid,' he replies, wiping the book with his sleeve.

I'm still smiling as I turn toward the steps of the restaurant. Then, just as I open the door, from the corner of my eye, I think I see a baby cobra sliding out from under the torn box. It slithers away into the darkness of the gutter leaving me to wonder if he'd told me the truth at all.

Hattie

Hattie had trawled countless dating websites but when she stumbled on something new her eyes lit up. She tapped the keys with expert precision, flicking crumbs and tiny pieces of bacon from the keyboard. She couldn't believe her luck. She mulled over the information as she headed into the kitchen and cut three giant slices of fresh bread, like doorsteps, and applied a heavy coating of peanut butter.

She sighed happily mulling it over. She'd always wanted to go to Barcelona but none of her friends were ever on holiday at the same time as her. The fast food restaurant where she worked didn't let staff have the same holidays although how Rach and Effie got the same two weeks holiday each year was a mystery.

Hattie protested to Micky the Supervisor but he waved her complaint away like he was swatting a fly so it meant that Hattie had to go on holiday alone again.

But now she'd found this website where she could actually stay on someone's sofa!

Perfect.

She was still licking the paste off her finger and picking bits from her teeth when she read a review posted by another solo traveller:

The first time I CouchSurfed solo, I went to Toronto in Canada. Two really nice guys collected me from the airport and drove me to their apartment. They had plenty of room and insisted I stay in their spare guest room. They cooked me dinner and suggested places for me to visit in the area. They gave me my own set of door keys so I could come and go. They were working the next day and told me to 'have a good day.' Since then I've stayed with hosts in Chile, Mexico and Thailand. AND I've also hosted foreign travellers myself from Spain. (Here's my profile.)

Hattie looked around her cramped kitchenette with the double bed pushed against the wall, an armchair and sofa where she sat, and a small dining table. But it did have a separate bathroom with a proper bath, she thought. There might be enough room for two people. I wouldn't mind. They could sleep on the couch. It could be quite fun having someone to stay. She would have to tidy up the place but it wouldn't take long to pick up the clothes and pop the remains of the last night's Chinese in the bin and her dirty clothes in a plastic bag to take to the laundrette.

She read the testimonial again. Her flat was well situated in the High Street. It was a blessing to live above the local Indian takeaway where rich and enticing herbs and spices wafted up to her each evening. In fact, it was a nice change to eat curried chips instead of the double cheeseburgers she ate for lunch most days. It was so handy just to be able to pop downstairs to get her dinner. Gergit often gave her extra poppadums.

Hattie swung her legs up onto the sofa. One of the perks of her job was to eat breakfast and dinner at work or, if she was on the late shift, it was lunch and dinner. She never had to cook which saved a lot of time and it meant that she could spend her free time meeting and chatting to people on the Internet.

Hattie had lots of friends. Three hundred and eighty-four on Facebook.

Now, encouraged that she could host foreigners from abroad, Hattie Googled: *Spanish men's names.*

She spent a couple of hours gazing at handsome images of soft, smooth olive skinned men, the type that Hattie liked so much, so different to her pale pallor.

Sometimes in the winter when she was cold her veins came to the surface causing her white skin to appear blotchy like a mottled mosaic. Her mother had passed a particularly nasty remark about her complexion last Christmas. She told Hattie not to have the extra portion of Christmas pudding but Hattie had been hungry. That had been right after Hattie's stepfather had thrown a turkey leg onto her plate - on top of her Christmas pudding and custard. It had ruined her meal. The turkey had tasted awful with custard on it. After dinner, Hattie's mother had taken a pair of scissors to Hattie's new jeans and she'd cut the seam saying Hattie would get into them now and then she'd laughed. She had been drunk again and had not noticed that Hattie was upset.

Wouldn't it be funny if I ended up marrying a Spaniard? Mum would sit up and take notice then.

Researching the Internet was thirsty work so Hattie opened a tin of coke and left it with the empty cans on the table. If she owned a can opener then she could make the empty can into a pencil holder. She had one biro that she'd nicked from work so she didn't really need a holder, so it wasn't worth all that effort.

Hattie yawned and stretched. She'd put on her pyjamas after she'd come home. They were much more comfortable that those tight black trousers she wore to work. They must have shrunk. They felt very tight. She'd have to get a new pair sometime.

Hattie scrolled and scanned the CouchSurf site.

This is easy. I can find common interests with strangers. She logged onto a forum and decided to send fifteen emails to different CouchSurf hosts living near Barcelona:

Hi – My name is Hattie. I'm twenty-three and live just outside London. I'm happy, fun and positive. I enjoy cinema and films.

Hattie paused, then read what another host had written and added to her text:

I've always wanted to go to Barcelona. I love to travel, meet new people and I want to learn about different cultures.

The fact she didn't know much about her own culture and she didn't even go into London, was not worth mentioning. It was too busy and there was never anywhere to sit. Although on the last occasion Hattie had gone to the West End, she'd found a clean spot on the pavement in Covent Garden. She'd rested there eating her sandwiches watching the world go by, as they stepped over her. She'd enjoyed that. She was a people watcher.

She read another host's profile, then she typed: *I love*

people watching.

Well, that bit is true.

She wandered to the fridge and raised the milk carton to her lips and left the box on the draining board beside the mugs and plates. She decided that while she was in the kitchen she would have some of the strawberry cheesecake she'd nicked from work. It was delicious. She cut a thick slice and with her mind on efficiency, she decided it would save her coming back if she just took a larger piece. She cut it in half.

She sat down with her plate and stared at the screen. She continued with her email:

I like cooking, food and I don't drink alcohol.

Now that had to be a point in her favour. She'd seen what it did to her Mum.

I eat a healthy diet.

A litre of milk, strawberries and cheese - wasn't that protein? Besides, bacon wasn't fattening like everyone said it was. There were loads of skinny people who ate bacon and cheese burgers. You just had to look at all the students who came into the restaurant.

It just goes to prove that scientists had it all wrong.

How did they do all their stupid research?

Hattie popped the last piece of cheesecake in her mouth and wiped her lips. She scrolled through the 'Find Hosts' and ticked the 'Want to Meet Up' box.

This will include meeting locals who aren't hosts, Hattie read aloud. Oh? I can write a message to anyone in the area that I would like to meet. *For best effect*, she read and licked her spoon, *include a specific request such as: I see that you love playing frisbee. I do too! Want to toss a disc around in a park?*

Hattie hated parks, too many dogs and children

running around. Besides she'd never thrown a Frisbee in her life. She thought hard and ten minutes later with the tap of a key she sent her emails. Hattie sat back. Feeling contented she burped loudly. It was just a touch of heartburn.

She liked to think of her messages sent from this tiny apartment in Essex going out through the airwaves across land and sea to strangers in Spain. She'd felt the same thrill when she started online dating with men in Russia, India and Malaysia.

They'd been heady days when she'd spent all night on the Internet. Once or twice she'd even missed work. But it was worth it. They were happy to talk to her. She'd used an old school photograph for her profile and they said she was very sexy and attractive. One man from Calcutta wanted to sleep with her. She'd sent money to another man in Turkey who wanted to learn English. He'd talked of marriage which had been exciting but then she'd never heard from him again. That had been two years ago and she'd learnt her lesson since then. No one was getting any money out of her now.

That's why she liked this CouchSurfing idea.

It was perfect.

She'd just made a mug of hot chocolate, eaten two digestives and placed six marsh mallows on a saucer when her laptop binged. She'd received a reply.

Hola Hattie, I live near Las Ramblas a busy and popular street. It's a one bedroom flat in the old town. I would like to welcome you as a guest to our home. When would you get here? Best regards Enrique.

***

Enrique - male or female?

She checked the host profile and photograph and smiled in satisfaction at his handsome serious face.

Hattie reread his message. Our home?

Wow!

Hello Enrique – Do you live alone? What do you do?

He replied immediately: *I live with my older brother. I am an engineering student and he is studying medicine. We like to meet and host foreign travellers. What about you?*

Hattie settled down behind the screen and dunked a marsh mallow into her chocolate. Then typed:

Hello Enrique, I could come over next week? How far are you from the airport?

He replied: *There is a bus but I could meet you at the airport?*

Hattie sighed and stood up. She had a stomach ache so she sat on the toilet thinking. What can I say to show myself in a good light and appear interesting? When she sat on the sofa ten minutes later, she typed:

I work in a restaurant. I haven't been to Spain before and I would like to learn Spanish.

Enrique replied immediately: *That's great. Are you a fully qualified chef? We like food and we both like to cook. We can teach you some Spanish but there are classes you can sign up to – if you want to. How long are you coming for?*

They can both cook!

Hattie laughed. She checked the length of an average stay on the CouchSurf site barely able to type with excitement. Her fingers tapped the wrong keys and the message took longer to write:

Perhaps a few days if that's alright? What Spanish food do you cook?

Enrique doesn't respond.

I bet he's making toast and marmite so Hattie wandered to the kitchen. It was past two o'clock and she yawned. Time goes so quickly chatting online. She browsed through the cupboards and eventually settled on Weetabix. She added milk and four heaped spoons of sugar and settled down in front of the screen again. She imagined a flat in Barcelona, bright, big and airy. It might even overlook the sea. I will lie on their white couch eating cheese on toast or making baked beans with Enrique.

Hattie and Enrique, she says aloud.

Enrique and Hattie.

She closed her eyes and saw a white wedding dress and a small chapel like the one in Mamma Mia. Her computer binged and Enrique's message is flagged:

That's fine. Let us know your dates and flight details. We can welcome you with a traditional paella when you arrive.

Paella?

What's that?

Hattie Googled paella and read: Eels, squid, crayfish, whelks and mussels.

Oh God!

A new message binged from Enrique:

We are very excited. Do you want to Skype?

Hattie closed the computer. She felt sick.

I need to give this CouchSurfing some more thought. It's not as simple as it appears. Perhaps I should start by thinking about the food and take it from there.

Maybe Indian? Chinese?

Probably American - ribs, burgers - that's safe.

Hattie was beginning to feel better already.

Jacob's Birthday

Millie fluffed up the pillows, straightened the duvet and looked around the bedroom. *Emma will be comfortable in here.* She pottered into the bathroom and ran the cloth around the sink for the fifth time and rubbed at an invisible smear on the mirror. *That will do or I'll rub it away.* On the landing she paused at the top of the stairs to listen. Jacob would be in the sunroom sitting in his favourite chair studying the daily cryptic crossword but she called out anyway: 'I'll be down in a minute. I'll just check Felicity's room.'

He didn't answer but then she didn't expect him to.

Although the girls were both mid-fifties with grown up families of their own, they were still her 'girls' – it didn't matter how old they were. She remembered them growing up in the house, running up and down the stairs and tears and tantrums if they hadn't been allowed to do something for one reason or another. It had all seemed hugely important at the time but now, like the faded vintage pattern on the wallpaper, it was almost forgotten. There had been colds and flu, a broken arm and a gash on

Emma's leg that had needed stitches and all through this when Millie had fussed around frantic and worried, Jacob had calmly taken over. He had bundled the girls into the car and taken them to the clinic or to a party or to a friend's house. He had always been their Knight and the girls adored him.

Millie sat on the bed and looked out of the window at the row of houses in the tree-lined street. The same view for over forty years. After Jacob got his first promotion at the law firm they celebrated with dinner at *The Ivy* and paid a substantial deposit on a four-bedroom house. It had been a home filled with laughter and tears, winter dinner parties around the long dining table, Easter egg hunts and summer barbecues on the pretty manicured lawn.

What was that? Did Jacob call?

Millie stood up and walked to the door. 'I'll only be a minute,' she called. 'Pop the kettle on – I'll be down in a moment.'

She returned to the bedroom and straightened the soft toys on the shelf. *Would Felicity remember Badger – her favourite panda bear?* She'd taken him when she went to University but when she moved to north Wales he had somehow mysteriously reappeared here, in her room. Badger's reappearance at home had coincided with the arrival of David who had gone with her to Wales. They now had two children and when they visited, they played with the trusted bear.

Although Millie loved her grandchildren they were not the same as her two girls – they were hers. They were a part of her. She remembered her pregnancy like it was yesterday and how in love she'd been.

Jacob called up the stairs again. He was impatient this

morning but she knew he was just as excited as she was. The girls would be here soon to celebrate his birthday - just the two of them. Felicity was driving from Llandudno and collecting Emma who lived just outside Oxford and they were staying for three nights.

Millie checked her appearance. Hollow eyes stared back at her so she smiled and the blue irises perked up revealing the beauty she'd once had as a young woman.

That's better!

She applied moisturiser, rubbing gently at her cheeks and neck enjoying the cool freshness against her skin, added mascara and pink blush, the same lipstick she had worn all her life.

'Pink lips,' Jacob had called her when they met the first time.

She had been twenty-one and they had sat together at a law school dinner. She had held her ground talking about equal rights, the starving in Africa and the closing of the mines in the north of England. He was charming, kind and attentive and Millie knew by the time the bread and butter pudding was served that this would be the man she would marry.

Jacob laughed when she had the courage to tell him after their wedding and he'd replied, 'Why did it take you so long to make up your mind? I knew the moment you sat down beside me.'

Millie smiled at the memory and checked her watch. The girls would be here soon, mid-day they said. She held the handrail as she negotiated the stairs. More recently they seemed steeper. Jacob always chided her on carrying things up the stairs and not holding on. She had slipped a few months ago and had broken a few ribs. She'd been lucky but it had been enough for Jacob to be concerned and for him to constantly remind her.

'I'm holding on to the banister, darling,' she called. 'Just as you always tell me.'

She peered in to the lounge. It was perfectly neat and tidy. Jacob was in his chair, head back, snoring softly with the crossword across his knees and the pen falling from his hand. He still had a good thick head of grey hair and he was wearing his favourite brown waistcoat with the mustard coloured shirt she'd bought for his birthday last year.

'I'll pop the kettle on then,' she said and turned toward the kitchen.

At almost eighty-three Millie didn't move as fast as she used to but she had plenty of time, almost an hour before her girls arrived.

She checked the fridge: smoked salmon, prawns, salad and avocado – Jacob's favourite. He had recently been diagnosed with diabetes and was watching his diet. She hadn't bought a cake this year. It wasn't life threatening but the doctor had prescribed daily medication. All in all, they had both been very lucky with their health. Hardly a day of illness between them, '*as tough as old boots*' he'd said on more than one occasion.

The kettle hissed and Millie lifted it from the gas. She poured boiling water over a tea bag and added a little milk then she sat at the kitchen table and contemplated the clock. The girls were on their journey, probably on the M40 near High Wycombe.

She reached for a pen and yesterday's newspaper. There were still three clues that she hadn't finished and they were annoying her. She tapped the paper with the pen and wondered if Jacob would know the answers. She'd ask him later. There was no point in disturbing him now. He'd been excited all week. The thought of the girls coming home had lifted his spirits.

'What are you buying all that shopping for?' he'd jested. 'Killing the fatted calf?'

'You're making apple tart - when you know I prefer sherry trifle?'

'They'll have to stay for a month to eat this lot.'

But Millie had ignored him.

She knew what was best for her girls. It was a shame they lived so far away. She'd often dreamed as they were growing up that they'd buy a house in the same street and would pop in for coffee. That they'd live close enough to meet on a Saturday or to go shopping when Jacob played golf.

But Felicity loved Wales and it was where she had her Vets Practice and Emma adored being near Oxford. John was a lawyer and in the early years after they married she'd hoped that Jacob would entice him toward London to be nearer to them but he didn't. Jacob was of the firm belief that everyone had to live their own lives and must walk their own path. He'd said that on many occasions.

'If he wants to come into my law firm, he's more than welcome but he's an ambitious man and his roots are elsewhere.'

But Millie never stopped hoping. She often wished they would move a little closer to her so that she would share their lives a little more.

Millie looked out of the window just as the Range Rover pulled up onto the gravel.

'They're here,' she shouted jumping up. 'They're here,

Jacob.'

'Alright, don't get so excited, pink lips. Look at you, jumping around like a giddy schoolgirl,' he replied.

'Have you done your hair?' She pulled him to her and ran her fingers across his fringe. 'Look at you, you need a haircut.'

Then she leaned against his shoulder, reassured by his strength, breathing in his familiar aftershave. It wasn't as strong as it usually was but then she felt his breath on her cheek and his soft lips as they met in a brief kiss.

'You're as excited as me,' she laughed.

He smoothed her hair from her forehead and placed a warm kiss on her cheek. 'Of course I am. They're our girls,' he whispered. 'Born out of my love for you.'

'Stop it, you big softie,' she chided. 'You'll have me crying in a moment.' She pulled away and tugged at her skirt smoothing it over her hips.

'You've lost far too much weight,' he said.

'I'll put it back on with the girls here.'

'You've enough food to feed a nation.'

'Come on, worry-chops!' Millie dropped his hand and opened the front door. 'Hello,' she called out and raised her hand to wave.

'Hi, Mum,' called Emma. She was the eldest by two years and she was the first to wrap her arms around her. 'Look at you! That's a pretty skirt - lilac was always your favourite colour.'

'Your Dad loves lilac,' she replied.

Emma had Jacob's green grey eyes and penetrating stare and like him, she felt Emma could see though her skin to her very soul. Emma frowned but it turned quickly into a warm smile and she stood aside.

Felicity was smaller and darker. She had a stocky-build more like Millie. As she embraced her tightly Millie was aware of her strong arms gripping her in a tight embrace.

'That's a bear hug,' she laughed.

Then she pulled both girls into her arms and the three of them hugged in the driveway. Millie was the first to pull away. She pulled a tissue from her pocket and turned to the house.

'Come inside,' she said leaving them with Jacob. She couldn't hog all the attention. She hurried into the kitchen and busied herself pulling out cups and saucers. Her movements were shaky and she put that down to emotion. *I mustn't ruin the moment.* She turned at the sound of footsteps following her and the girls dumping their holdalls on the hallway floor.

'You must be gasping after that journey. Coffee? Tea? Was it busy? Were the roads okay?'

'No problem.' Emma stalked around the kitchen taking everything in, as if seeing changes although nothing had altered, perhaps she had her own memories. She leaned against the sink and then gazed out at the garden. 'Goodness, Mum, what a windfall, those apples need collecting.'

'I was hoping you'd take some back – there're far too many for us…'

'I'll collect them after lunch.' Felicity stood beside them. 'Do you remember how we used to make chutney together? Dad's recipe was the best…'

'The leaves are turning – we'll be changing the clocks soon.' Mille sighed. She hated the winter; dark nights, cold and damp days.

This won't do!

She fussed around the girls, settling them in to the family home, chatting and laughing. They picked up framed photographs on top of the mantelpiece and exclaimed about the years that passed so quickly and how the children have grown. Millie had always been careful to have the same amount of photographs of them and their children. The girls had always been treated the same: equally and fairly. It was something that she and Jacob had prided themselves on.

Now, after the initial euphoria of their arrival, Jacob retired to finish the crossword in the sunroom leaving his three girls to chat at the table and to drink coffee.

'So what will we do for Dad's birthday tomorrow?' Emma's eyes glistening in excitement.

'Lunch in Dean's?' suggested Felicity. 'I could book a table?'

'Dean's isn't as good as it used to be so I bought some prawns and salmon to have at home.' Millie topped up their coffee cups.

'Really?' Felicity looked disappointed.

'But it would make a change to go out, Mum?' She felt that Emma looked right through her. 'It would save all this hassle at home.'

'It's no trouble. It's whatever you girls would like to do. I just thought it would be nice to eat at home.'

'Where did you get the fish from?' Felicity asked.

'Waitrose.' Millie turned away. She hated it when the girls started asking too many questions. She just wanted them to relax and have fun and now they were questioning her.

'But we wanted to take you out.' Felicity shared a look with Emma.

Millie shifted uncomfortably in her seat. She was determined not to be flustered so she sipped her coffee slowly and said:

'I've made an apple tart.' She wanted them to know that she had gone to a lot of effort for them. She had been baking all week. It had kept her busy and Jacob loved her home cooking. 'It'll be far tastier than anything you get out in a restaurant.'

'But it's Dad's birthday and we want to celebrate…' Felicity couldn't hide the frustration in her voice.

'He loves apple tart,' Millie replied.

Emma reached across the table and placed her hand on top of her mother's. 'Are you alright?'

'I'm fine. Just happy to see you both.' She spoke slowly to keep her voice under control, willing her eyes not to fill with tears.

'Are you very lonely?' Felicity whispered taking her mother's other hand.

It took Millie a while to hold back her tears and to control her voice. 'There's not a day I don't think of him.'

'We're here now,' Emma said.

'We love you,' added Felicity.

Millie stared back at her two daughters and was reminded of Jacob. She was filled with a love so sharp that it sliced through her heart, splitting her soul. She could barely speak. She swallowed the swell of sadness that rose in her gut like a giant wave, then swallowed again and again until the tsunami subsided and she was able to speak again.

'You're both here and that's all that matters,' she said.

Just A Drag

The first drag makes my head spin. It was always the worst. It's the one I pretend never affects me. After that my body kicks in and accepts the crazy nicotine that calms me yet sets my adrenalin galloping faster than Usain Bolt on speed. I spit out a bit of tobacco leaf. That's the problem with roll-ups. Unless I twist the end really tight, I end up chewing the stuff like I'm a cowboy: Clint Eastwood or John Wayne.

But I'm not that type of bloke. I'm an ordinary guy, medium build, medium everything. I hunch my shoulders and dig my chin into the collar of my leather jacket and edge further behind the wall, out of the wind and out of sight. I still had seven minutes to go until I had to be at my desk and like Shylock, they weren't getting another pound of flesh from me. I worked hard enough.

On my second drag I blow a smoke ring and it clusters in fluffy, grey angelic halos so I blow another because there's nothing else to do. Then Angie's voice floats from the open window beside where I'm standing.

'I'm telling you Miles, don't do anything, or say anything. Don't panic. I'll get rid of them.' Her tone is soothing and I smile. I like Angie. She has the same calming tune to her voice that she used to the new trainee last week.

Was it Simon? Steve? I can't remember his name. They come and go. He'd only lasted a day. That's the nature of a call centre, she once told me in her purring voice. But he'd said he couldn't stand cold calling. He said it wasn't right.

It sounds like Angie is on the phone and I feel uncomfortable listening but I've still got another few minutes. I wasn't going to waste my roll-up.

'I'll get another name for you today. Just be more careful and don't make any mistakes this time. Did you clear up after yourself?' she asks.

When I first started working here I couldn't take my eyes off Angie. She's the supervisor - the boss - I was drawn to her pale skin and the large freckle at the top of her left breast. My eyes were like magnets to that mole. At first I thought it was a brown smear or smudge of makeup. Then I thought it was a small tattoo of one of those long Greek islands, then some days I can't make up my mind. But I know really that it's just a freckle.

I take another gulp of nicotine and stamp my feet to keep the chill from my toes in my worn trainers. You'd have thought a guy my age would wear sensible shoes and I would, if I could afford them.

Angie's voice has an edge to it – one that I've never heard before but she's moved away from the window and is walking around her office so I can't hear what she's saying.

Normally when she trains us, she's funny, friendly and polite.

'*Smile when you're speaking on the phone,*' she reminds us each day. '*Even though people can't see you, they can still hear you and they will hear the smile and laughter in your voice. It will give them confidence. They will believe in you. They will like you and they will trust you.*'

I'm not the only one who fancies her.

There are boys much younger and far more agile working on the team. They are braver than me. They've even tried it on with her and she flirts back. She's good at that. She handles them well. She laughs off their advances with a pat to their six-pack or a squeeze of their bicep. Sometimes she ruffles their hair or taps their cheek but with me she's different.

I guess it's because I'm older and I'm married. I'm not as enthusiastic as the young bucks and they make me smile. Half the time I stroll around with a nonchalant smile on my lips. I won't be turned down or patronised or made a fool of and she knows this. Sometimes she gives me a playful wink over their heads or across one of the computer screens that separate our workstations.

It's a complicit look. It's one that says: see how I put up with these guys? See how I handle them? But I love it!

Sometimes I nod back. I'm flattered that she singles me out. I'm different. She feels safe with me. She trusts me.

Alan, one of the young bucks, said it was because I was an old codger. He said that she feels sorry for me but I know that's not true.

Angie values me. She took me into her office only last week and said she appreciated the research I was doing. Many people my age would find it a drag going to work but I told her I love it. Angie also said, I was good at my job and that I might get a fat bonus at Christmas.

I hug my bomber jacket closer to my chest and inhale deeply from the minuscule butt just as Angie raises her voice.

'I can't keep taking this risk, especially if you're going to bugger everything up.'

Shocked.

I tilt my head. I've never heard Angie swear before and it brings a smile to my face, she's got grit, so I move closer to the window and risk a quick peak inside.

Her hair is long and lustrous as if she's washed it in some magical oil that makes it shine. Her profile shows a stubby nose and a determined chin. She leans over her desk, her short blue dress barely covering her arse and her long legs disappearing into infinity. Golden bangles clatter on her wrist as she writes, then she pushes the tip of the pen between her purple-coloured lips concentrating on a computer print-out like the ones she allocates to us each day. She monitors all our calls, the names of the people and phone numbers.

Alan reckons Angie is a still water and runs deeper than we think. He thinks there's another side to her and she isn't all she seems. He thinks she's putting on an act. He called her a tiger but he's probably got some sexy fantasy going on in his head.

'Look, I'll give you another one but this time do it properly!'

She runs her eyes down the list and if I stand on tiptoe I see the list is the one from yesterday. It has been highlighted with yellow and pink marker pens.

'Erm, let's see, this one. This isn't too far. It's Ashford,' she pauses, stands up and scratches her scalp with the biro. 'It's an hour. Anything closer might be suspicious. We agreed two or three hours, max. What about Margate?'

I bring the fag to my lips wondering if I have time to roll another. Smoke rises and stings my eyes and when I rub them they fill up and feel sore and prickly.

Margate would be two hours from here easily. That's a long way for whatever it is.

'This one is out all afternoon. There's someone in after five.'

I bounce up and down on my heels. That wind is fresh today. Angie must be on to Graham arranging appointments.

Hang on?

Hadn't she called him Miles?

I thought it was Graham who organised the salesmen's visits. I wonder if he's left. I liked Graham. He was decent, and more importantly, he had a nice way with the old dears on the phone. He always told the sales guys to call first so as not to alarm the old folk. They may be having a nap or watching TV or something, so it was always best to call twenty minutes earlier. *They can pop the kettle on,* he said. When Graham gave us the sales course he said, 'It's important that people *like* you. If they won't buy you a coffee or make you a tea it's because they don't like you and no-one, no-one,' he stressed, 'would buy anything from you. Not if they didn't like you. Double-glazing or not. It didn't matter, and old folk could get a real bee in their bonnet. If you messed up then the guys like me, the guys in telesales, suffered because their commission went down.'

I'd never understood the ins and outs of business but

that had made sense and again, like Angie and because I was older, he had singled me out for a nod of the head and a wink. When the training was over, he had slapped me on the shoulder saying he wished there were older folk like me with gumption and stamina to go out to work.

'56 Mooreton Road,' Angie's voice floats past me.

I stop bouncing.

That address rings a bell. I peer through the window, the butt of my cigarette burns my fingers. I curse silently.

'Yes, Mooreton Road. M – O – O...' Angie hoops glossy hair behind her pixie ear and like most of the boys in the office, I have also thought about kissing those ear lobes. I'm taking the final drag from my butt. It's almost time to start work and I move away from the window, cough and bring up phlegm.

'Mrs Childer,' she says.

Mrs Childer is my client. I called her yesterday. Had she lived in Margate? She'd said she was going to London all this week but she would be back on Sunday.

I hope Angie wasn't making a mistake. She was on the 'call again to confirm next week's list.'

I blow out the smoke. The acrid taste is strong and it makes me want a coffee but I return and stand in my place under the window. I want to have my facts straight, then I can tell Angie she's made a mistake. I'll tell her the truth; that I was having a fag before work and I overheard her.

I check my watch. I've three minutes until I have to be at my desk.

'Look Miles, if you're going to screw up, I'll find someone else.'

So it was Miles and not Graham she's talking to.

'Don't tell a soul. I don't care that he's done jobs with you before. This is for you to do alone. So get on with it!'

Miles?

He must be one of the new sales reps. He must have been shadowing one of the more experienced sales men and now she wants him to do this job on his own. I'm surprised that Angie is so heavily involved with the sales reps' visits. She always said she had nothing to do with them and that they were always planned via the head office 'up north.'

'I Googled it. It's behind a bloody great hedge.'

Angie really does her homework – she's thorough. It sounds like Miles hasn't got a great amount of experience but he would soon get better. The company is really hot on training. I've lost count of all the courses I've had in the past month.

'I'll destroy it. They'll never know. Text me when you get there. It looks massive.'

That's kind of Angie to offer support. There would be a lot of windows. That's why we target so many of the older population. Statistics show that they invariably live in old houses that need upgrading or modernising and they have the disposable income. It's our job to get them to spend money on renovating their homes. It's good insulation and it will keep them warm and reduce their heating bills. I couldn't cold-call old folk if I thought it wouldn't benefit them – it wouldn't be fair.

'And make sure you wipe it clean.' Angie's voice is harsher than I expect.

I stand on tiptoe and she's tapping the biro on my print-out sheet.

Angie is kind like that. She never seems to mind that I

don't make appointments or that I don't know when the old folk are in but I *do* know when they are out. I engage them in small talk and they always want to tell me when they're going out or if they're going away. I remember what Graham said – be kind and take an interest and it's easy for me I've got all the time in the world.

I decide to roll another cigarette so it's ready for my mid-morning break. It saves time and I'll be able to bring my coffee outside and have a few minutes longer – perhaps time for two smokes.

Mrs Childer is away this week. I'll have to tell Angie not to send Miles or any other salesman round, especially if they are going to travel all the way to Margate.

Then it all begins to make sense. Of course, Miles is replacing the windows with double glazing. It's a big house, so maybe they've already got the contract if she's telling this Miles chap to 'wipe it clean.'

Fingerprints can leave terrible smears.

I pop the new roll up behind my ear.

That was a quick sale. On Monday Mrs Childer was enthusiastic about her trip to London. She must have cancelled it and arranged to have double glazing installed over the weekend. She must have liked me a lot. I wonder which salesman went to see her and if I'll get any commission. She was my client.

Angie said I might get an extra bonus at Christmas so it's probably best I don't say anything. I won't cause a fuss. I'm sure a company this size has it all under control.

It's one minute to nine when I slip inside and sit at my desk. I switch on my computer, ignoring the banter from the team around me thinking I might buy a steak pie tonight and a bottle of wine to celebrate.

Angie leans against her office door holding a new computer print out and she singles me out for a smile. She really is a kind-hearted soul and I like her more each day. A lot of people call this job a real drag but I think I'm good at it.

'Morning Angie.' I tilt my cap at her and smile. I'm ready for another busy day of phone calls. She places the list on my desk and for some reason today, as she bends over me, her freckle looks remarkably like Corfu.

I'd Lie In The Road For You

'I'd lie in the road for you,' she said.

I was never sure if Auntie Marjorie actually meant it or if she was just joking and I never found out. Sadly, a year later Marjorie was knocked down by a truck in Spain and she died.

I missed her.

She was bright and funny and she'd often said silly things to me: 'You're like a tadpole jumping in and out of the water all day.'

I'd replied:

'How could I look like a tadpole? I'm a fifty year old with cellulite, and besides paddling in the sea with my trouser legs rolled up hardly constituted jumping in and out.'

I never went back to Spain and ironically I started speaking to her much more after she died. I didn't have to bother with a phone or Skype and it was much easier to walk Mitzy and gaze up at the stars and imagine Marjorie in heaven looking down on us.

In the woods, by the sea or up on the Downs where it's quiet. It didn't matter. Sometimes in winter when the evenings were darker I'd wait for a break in the cloud to spot a shining star and I'd imagine it was her, up there, with her twinkling eyes laughing at me as I sheltered from the rain.

'Silly sod, you should have put on a warm hat, a tea cosy would do - it would be an improvement,' she'd tease.

Then it was Trevor's turn.

I began to speak to him almost the day he died - even before the funeral. Trevor was my husband's brother. Cancer took him at the age of forty-two. We nursed him, well - I did. Toward the end I'd spoon fed him and told him the cricket results.

'Kent won,' I'd say and I'd read to him how many runs, ducks and overs there had been. It meant nothing to me but a lot to him. I got quite used to looking at the scores and commenting on the players. I liked the anticipation of his interest and his happiness in what I was saying. I missed it.

My ex travelled to India after Trevor died. He said he couldn't cope and had to have some time out. That's when he became my ex. It turned out that I didn't miss him at all in India.

It was Trevor who stayed in my heart. He understood me more than his brother ever did. He'd always been kind and I enjoyed looking after him. We talked about anything and everything. He never laughed at me or judged me. He just listened and nodded and said things would always work out - and they do.

Most days I look up at the sky and speak to him.

'You know what Trevor? Today is easier. I don't feel as

low as yesterday.'

I always tried to tell him good news, something positive and optimistic. He'd been so poorly toward the end but now I imagine him happy and laughing up there with Aunt Marjorie, sharing a whiskey nightcap and a joke and probably even the cricket results - she liked the game too.

'He's a fine looking chap,' Marjorie told me one evening when I was searching for Mitzy who'd disappeared nose first into a rabbit hole. A light was twinkling in the night sky and I paused to look up at her.

'She's a lovely nutcase,' Trevor replied. His star was also shining brightly, right beside hers.

I scanned the ground and eventually found Mitzy and put her on the lead.

That's when I thought about Dolly. We had been at school together. We'd grown up in the same street and we'd gone to the same school. We were closer than sisters but when she married Frank I was as surprised as the next person. She'd never shown any interest in him. He was a wide-boy, always on the make and money was king but Dolly went along with it all and when the children came along I think she turned a blind eye to his wandering eye and the ladies who made him laugh out loud.

I saw him once. He was snuggled in the corner of a pub whispering into the ear of a girl, younger than his daughter. I saw the way his hand travelled up her skirt. I probably should have said something to him but I didn't. I didn't tell Dolly either. Dolly didn't need me to tell her what he was like.

There were plenty of people around here who'd do that.

At first Dolly had laughed it off. Then she began to look

tired and withdrawn and after going to the doctors she was manically happy again. I said I wanted some of those happy pills she was taking and she'd looked at me for a fraction of a second with very sad eyes before bursting into laughter and the moment was past.

Gone.

Then so was Dolly.

Two days later.

Frank found her hanging in the garage.

It's hard not to look up at the sky and imagine Dolly suspended from the stars, dangling, swaying, laughing and saying, 'these happy pills are fantastic you should try them.'

So when I take Mitzy out I'm never really alone. There's always Marjorie, Trevor or Dolly.

I chat away with them all. I ask them their opinion. Just like I did yesterday again. It's been on my mind for so long and it's affected me so much that I've been on sick leave from the bank for a few months now.

It isn't like me to be ill but these youngsters come in with their big ideas for change and training courses filled with ambition and motivated by careers and quite frankly I'm tired of it all. It's like I've been left behind. My energy and youthful positive zest has been replaced by keeping up to date, to learn quicker ways to get a job done.

My supervisor is twenty years younger than me but I'm paid more than her because of my length of service. I know it seems wrong and I would feel guilty but she's so nasty to me I don't feel any guilt at all. I only feel the bubbling of her hatred and bullying attitude and it causes me to shake and my body rattles in my own skin like I'm permanently cold.

I walk Mitzy and I look up. I ask my friends up there, what I should do?

'Spill hot soup over her?' Marjorie suggests.

I shake my head. The days when that would make me laugh seem over.

Dolly who has known me longer than anyone is always in two minds. She can never decide. Eventually she says, 'Take her out for a drink and tell her what a shit she is. Then, after you've cleared the air, you'll feel better.'

'But that could make things worse,' I argue with the twinkling star.

'Then put up or shut up. Leave! There're more jobs out there. Don't stress it.'

I know Dolly is right.

Trevor always gives sensible advice. 'Go to your line manager. Tell them how you feel and how she overlooks your contribution in meetings or is constantly nagging at the way you do things. Get your job description clarified.'

I smile up at him. He's the star that shines the brightest.

I'm only human. It keeps me awake at night.

I went back to work and I said nothing.

I have a busy head and it's my undoing because each day gets worse. I'm good for nothing. I'm constantly tired and I find it hard to concentrate.

My supervisor said, 'Maybe you've come back to work too early.'

The next day she said, 'Maybe you need a refresher course.'

And yesterday. 'If this continues I'll have to report it. There will be an investigation.'

That's when I shake even more. It's like I rattle when I walk. My frame is fragile and I think my knees might collapse. So I take Mitzy out and up onto the heath.

I gaze up at the stars but it hurts my neck so I lay down to look at The Plough. The grass is wet under my head, my back and my bottom but it's comforting to feel the damp earth soaking into my body. Mitzy must like it too because after licking my face she settles under my arm for a snuggle.

I say: 'So, Marjorie, are you awake up there?'

'Of course I am, tadpole. What you need is a holiday. You don't need to put yourself through all of this nonsense.'

'What's it all about? What's it all for?' I ask.

'Just carry on what you're doing and it will all work out. They'll see she's some little upstart and soon get rid of her.'

'They're promoting her,' I reply.

'Oh well, maybe she'll move from your department.'

'My new supervisor is only twenty-five. She's heading for the top.'

'That's understandable - she's young,' Trevor interrupts. 'There's nothing wrong with ambition.'

'Why does it have to make you so unkind?' I whisper.

'It's power. It's a heady mix. Some people can't handle it and it goes to their head,' he replies.

'But these people are ruthless. Is this what life is about?' I squeeze my eyes closed. I don't want them to see my tears.

'It is for them. Perhaps you should take up a hobby and focus your energy on other things.'

'Like cricket?' I smile. 'It used to be fun when I read you articles from the newspaper and you explained what a *googlie* was.'

His laugh rumbles across the sky like thunder.

'Bugger that,' says Dolly. 'Tell your supervisor that you're not putting up with some young kid bossing you around. Demand they send you on a course, brush up your skills. Fight back.'

'I haven't got the same energy I had at thirty. I'm too tired.'

'Well then, say nothing and do as little as possible and look for an early retirement package.' She folds her arms angrily. I'm not in favour of her contribution.

'They don't do those packages any more. I'm stuck in this job forever. How they expect people to go on working until they're 68 – soon it will be 70 or 80? We should strike. It shouldn't be allowed. We should stand up to our government, shouldn't we?'

No-one answers and a fingernail moon appears like a sliver of cut glass from behind an ink-coloured cloud.

'What's it like to do nothing all day?' I ask them.

'I travel all the time.' Marjorie's voice tells me she's smiling. 'I can visit anyone and see what they're doing. I can go to any country and watch the sunrise or sunset. I can fly with the eagles, sing with the birds, gallop with wildebeests and visit my family. I watch them grow.'

'It's very quiet here,' says Trevor.

'But you can watch the cricket whenever you like now - can't you travel to Australia or India?'

'It's not the same as touching a rose petal, smelling a freshly cut lawn or holding the hand of someone you love.'

'Is that what you miss?'

'I miss the human touch. The softness of skin and making love-'

'Dirty git!' Dolly laughs. 'You're like Frank. He couldn't keep his hands off the girls. He still can't. His latest has just dumped him. He buys them expensive gifts and then complains they overspend. Then they argue. Same old pattern - they take him for a ride – and I'm not talking sex.'

Mitzy cuddles into the crook of my arm. She's lovely and warm. Her heart is beating against my arm in small rhythmic bumps like she's trying to keep up with my heart.

What would I miss if I died?

'It wouldn't be so bad if you stopped avoiding the real issue,' says Dolly interrupting my busy head, 'the main problem that you refuse to face.'

'Go away.' I breathe in Mitzy's doggy scent and hide my face in her fur.

'You bury your head in the sand all the time. You always have-'

'He still loves you,' interjects Marjorie. 'He never stopped loving you.'

'I don't know how you don't see it, dopey cow,' adds Dolly. 'He keeps phoning you, doesn't he?'

'Yes.' My voice is hoarse.

'He's back from India now. He says he's found himself and he's over it all. Didn't he say he forgives you? You know he wants you back, don't you?' insists Dolly.

'But I let him down. I don't deserve him.' Mitzy struggles from my grip.

'You do,' says Marjorie. 'You were together for over thirty years. He loves you and you love him. You were made for each other.'

'We couldn't have been otherwise how could have what happened – happen?'

'It was a cloud on a summer's day. Nothing more or less. Don't make it out to be so important.'

'But it was important,' says Trevor angrily. 'It was real.'

'Trevor needed you and you became dependent on each other. Emotionally attached,' explains Marjorie.

'If we'd been happy then it wouldn't have happened,' I repeat and curl on my side trying to make sense of it all and ignoring the damp seeping into my clothes.

'It happens in life but if he wants you back-'

'Don't you understand?' I shout at the stars. 'I haven't forgiven myself. I let him down. He was worth so much more than that-'

'He wants you back.'

I turn to look up at Marjorie twinkling in the sky. 'Should I go?'

'Yes,' says Dolly.

'Definitely,' says Marjorie.

'Trevor?'

He doesn't answer.

'Am I'm letting you down?'

The clouds gather into a dark blanket that covers the sky. He still doesn't reply. How easy it would be to lay back in the earth and let it swallow me up. I could sink like quicksand into the ground. Earth to earth. Could I just stop breathing? Can I stop my heart from beating? What if I never moved again?

'Get up you silly cow, you'll catch cold – probably pneumonia. No one will want a sick old biddy.' Dolly's voice floats over me.

'It's time to go home.'

Beside me Mitzy stretches and yawns and above our heads the clouds part to reveal Orion's plotted course and it shines like choreographed diamond steps.

'Trevor, what do you think?'

He stays silent.

'Trevor!' I shout. 'Trevor?'

I dust down my jeans and brush the wet grass from my jacket, straighten my bobble hat and pick up Mitzy's lead. 'Come on, sweetie. Let's go home.'

Wind rustles through the trees and whips around my ears and the faint whisper of Trevor's voice is carried on the undulating air and I pause to look up to make sure I hear him properly.

'I'd lie in the road for you,' he says. 'But he's your husband.'

The Bar

The bar is full. The Spanish hotel seems to have the normal mix of people: holidaymakers, business travellers, golfers - and me. It's five star, situated on the Mediterranean and the bar where I'm sitting overlooks the pretty bay.

It suits me perfectly.

It attracts a decent class of people who aren't interested in free drinks, happy hour or an all-inclusive tariff. A professional waiter balances a tray with one arm behind his back and pours expensive gin from the bottle over glistening ice cubes with a slice of lime. Not an optic in sight. He places bowls of nibbles on the table: nuts, sunflower seeds and salted crisps.

This is the part I like best.

I'm sitting on a high stool and the decorative mirror behind the bar allows me to see over my shoulder; who comes in and who goes out, who looks interesting and who has a story to tell.

I prefer older, mature company. They invariably have

more confidence and a similar outlook of the world to mine. I like conversations and discussions with strangers and enjoy them more if they're eye-candy - foreign or exotic-looking.

It feeds my imagination and stirs my excitement.

I feign interest in *The Alchemist* lying open and face down at my elbow, my mobile phone lies inert on the bar. I don't want to appear that I'm waiting for anyone special.

I look up as a group of Scandinavian golfers jostle for position at the bar and take my first sip of gin, allowing the ice cubes to bounce off my teeth and the lime to touch my tongue.

Ummm.

It's easy to spot a foreigner – especially a golfer – the colour co-ordinated clothing and V-necked jumpers give them away. For example, there are two men who stand nearer to me and slightly to one side of this group. The smaller man is wearing olive green trousers and a checked white and brown shirt, his jumper draped casually across his shoulders. By contrast the taller man wears pink trousers and a red jumper and because of his white hair I find him more distinguished and definitely interesting.

I cross my legs and watch them in the mirror.

It doesn't take them long to attract the attention of the waiter and order drinks - or to notice me. Although it's not cold I've worn black tights and my short skirt, after I cross my legs, has risen up my thigh. At the moment my cleavage remains covered by a lilac shawl over my low-cut purple dress and I toss my blond hair over my shoulder and look the other way.

Once their drinks are ordered they turn their back to the bar and survey the scene. They lean closer together pretending to talk golf or business but they're secretly studying the women: a beautiful Iranian girl with her boyfriend sitting near the window, a plain woman with two children, and an older woman who sits staring into space beside a man she has begun to look like; grey hair and denim shirts.

When the golfers turn their attention to me I happen to look up and I smile.

'Hello,' the taller distinguished man says. He raises his glass. He's the flirter one. His cheeks are soft and I think I can even smell his aftershave. He's my type of man. His blue eyes shine and crinkle in delight even though he's pretending not to look at my thigh.

'Good evening.' I raise my glass in salute.

The small man leans forward to see who his friend has spoken to and he grins at me. They've ordered gin and tonics too. It's all quite civilised.

'Cheers!' He raises his glass to me then looks up at his friend and smiles.

'Salud.' I reply. My phone becomes suddenly interesting. I tap out a message and tilt my head so that the men can see my profile and the beauty spot on my left cheek. My hair, recently shaped and blow-dried, tumbles onto my shoulders and emphasises my carefully applied makeup. My lipstick is a perfect lilac to match my shawl. I frown, tilt my mobile toward the light and utter a small groan leaving my shawl to fall slightly from my shoulder.

'Can't you get a reception?' says the tall man.

'I did – it seems to come and go.'

He nods and pops a sunflower seed into his mouth.

'Like the tide,' I add.

'Ha, yes, the sea, of course,' he pauses. 'Where are you

from?'

'London,' I lie Everyone loves the capital. Most people have visited.

'Ah…a beautiful city-'

'And you?'

'Sweden.'

'A lovely country,' I smile.

'You've been there?'

'I've been to Stockholm a few times.'

'I live a little north of there.'

'Beautiful.' I widen my smile and look interested.

He takes a step closer and leans on the bar near my elbow. 'Are you on holiday?'

I flip my hand. 'A bit of both – holiday and work.'

He raises his eyebrows and looks impressed.

The smaller man, not to be out done, picks up his drink and walks boldly to my other side. 'Are you waiting for someone?'

'I was, but they just texted me to say their plane is delayed.'

'Your husband?'

'I haven't spoken to my ex husband in five years.'

They join in with my laughter and the taller man with pink trousers moves closer to my shoulder.

'It's my business partner,' I explain. 'She was catching a later flight but she's missed it.' I place the mobile on the bar. 'Oh well, she'll be here tomorrow morning for our meeting – that's the main thing.'

'We've just arrived,' explains the smaller man inching closer.

'To play golf?' I ask.

His eyes are deep set and serious. I guess he is probably

an accountant back in his native country.

He nods. 'Do you play?'

'Yes, but not on this trip.'

The tall man takes surreptitious glances at me, eats another nut and sips his gin.

'It's a shame your business partner isn't here.' The small man looks meaningfully at the taller man. It's a look that says, we might all have had dinner together.

'These things happen.' I sip my gin and smile at the taller man.

'What business do you have?' He's thoughtful and calm. I guess he's probably a lawyer.

'Interiors. I'm a designer. I import fixtures and fittings…'

'Do you own a shop?'

'I supply small shops – the ones that charge a fortune in the marina,' I laugh.

The tall man checks out my jewellery, earrings, gold bangles and discreet rings. I reposition myself on the stool, pulling my shawl to cover myself but I manage to reveal my enhanced breasts.

The smaller man finishes his drink and rattles the cubes. He utters something in Swedish but his friend doesn't respond, instead he pops another nut in his mouth and seems to consider while the smaller man puts his hands in his pockets and rocks on his feet.

I pick up my book.

'Would you like a drink?' asks the smaller man.

'That's kind – thank you.' I place my book to one side. *The Alchemist* can wait. He summons the waiter and orders three more gins.

'Where are you playing golf?'

They list some courses and I nod – yes of course, I've heard of them – and yes, I think Tiger Woods has lost the edge and no I missed the Open but I do like Rory McIlroy. The Swedish golfer? Who? No – I don't know him…

'So what hobbies do you have?' The smaller man tells me his name is Nikki.

'I like walking and gardening.'

'Do you sail?' asks Erik, the distinguished man.

They're standing one each side of me and I defer my attention to them both equally, so neither feels excluded, and occasionally my gaze lingers on Erik in the mirror. Sometimes his deep blue eyes fleetingly meet mine and I wonder what he's thinking. He's a challenge and I like that.

'I love the water but no, I wouldn't know one end of a boat from the other; stern and aft or something?'

Erik smiles. His lips are full and and he pouts comically.

Nikki says. 'We could rent a boat when your friend comes over. If you could get a couple of hours free from your work. There are dolphins out there…'

'Really? I'd love to see them-'

Erik signals the waiter for another round of drinks and Nikki's hand rests on the back of my bar stool. Occasionally his palm brushes my shoulder.

I pull my shawl over my shoulders allowing them a flash of my brown breasts. 'But aren't you playing golf everyday?' I ask.

Nikki says something in Swedish and when I look in the mirror Erik winks at me.

A few minutes later when Nikki disappears to the toilet, Erik taps my glass with his. He leans closer to my ear and his breath is sweet on my cheek. I imagine his kiss would be soft and persistent and he whispers. 'It's a pleasure to meet you, Marcia.'

'And you, Erik.'

His rests his fingers lightly on my knee and his touch sends the skin on my arm into goose bumps. 'Look what you've done,' I laugh.

He traces my hand and my wrist with the back of his index finger. 'Oh dear!'

We both laugh.

'I don't think I should have any more to drink. I was waiting to have dinner with Sheila but now she's not coming, I'll…'

'We could have dinner together,' Erik suggests just as Nikki returns He overhears and says. 'Shall we eat in the hotel or go out?'

Erik looks away. His attention strays to a long limbed redhead who joins her boyfriend at a nearby table.

Nikki speaks in Swedish but Erik doesn't reply. He pops another nut in his mouth and seems to consider his answer.

I pick up my book and make to leave. 'I should leave you men to eat dinner on your own. It's the first night of your holiday, I'm sure you don't want me-'

'I don't want you to eat with him on my own,' says Nikki laughing. 'Come with us. What do you fancy? Steak, fish, pasta?'

'It would be lovely to have company. I wasn't looking forward to an evening on my own…but only if you're sure I won't be interrupting…'

Erik smiles. 'It would be a pleasure.'

Nikki's fingers trail across my back in a rotating

massage as Erik leans across the bar and asks the waiter about a restaurant close to the hotel.

'It would be easier to eat here,' says Nikki. His touch is gauche and his fingers smaller.

I say, 'But what would your wives say about you eating dinner with a foreign woman you met in a hotel?' I giggle - the gin is taking effect - and I'm feeling good.

Nikki blushes and pretends to slip his wedding band off his finger.

Erik shrugs. 'We're on our holiday. Boys can be naughty when they go away.'

'Really?'

Erik shrugs. 'Why not?'

'One more before dinner?' Nikki suggests and leans across the bar to attract the waiter's attention. In this split second Erik's finger moves to my thigh and his hand slides under my skirt. His finger is gentle and it's over in a second. But it's enough to make me want him.

When Nikki turns around he knows something has passed between us but we all clink glasses and toast in Swedish, English and Spanish.

Nikki's arm rests on my shoulder and Erik's thigh is pressed against my knee. Occasionally his fingers trace the underside of my thigh and we're giggling drunkenly at the Swedish they are teaching me. *I love you* – and - *I want you* – but - *come to my room* – is much harder to pronounce.

'I must visit the Ladies before dinner.' I pick up my book and mobile and place them in my bag. 'I won't be long.'

'We'll wait for you outside the dining room.'

'Lovely.' I slide from the bar stool and totter toward the reception but instead of turning left to the Ladies, I turn right. In a few seconds I'm outside. I walk briskly laughing at the fun we'd had. Steak would have been nice but-

Within five minutes I'm home. I take the lift up to the apartment which is dark and airless. I kick off my shoes and head into the lounge.

Dan is watching television and he barely looks up.

'Are you alright, honey?' I ask.

He grunts.

'Sorry I'm late. I met some friends.'

He blinks.

'Tonight I was a businesswoman from London. I think next week I might be an off duty policewoman – what do you think?'

Spit dribbles from the corner of his mouth and I bend down and reach for a tissue and wipe it away.

'It's only a harmless bit of fun but it beats being a nurse for a couple of hours.' I kiss his forehead. He's so much better looking that the two Swedish men. 'I thought we'd have stew for dinner, my darling. I hope you're hungry?'

As usual he doesn't reply.

I turn his wheelchair toward the kitchen. Since the motorcycle accident his brain is damaged. He doesn't understand much of what I say and he can't concentrate for long. It would be another long evening but at least it was fun in the bar tonight.

Jan d'Artagnan

I join the group of strangers standing in the hallway waiting for the soccer game in the gym to finish.

'Are you here for the class?' I ask a blond woman almost a decade older than me.

She's leaning against the wall, arms folded, watching the door. Her eyes narrow and she looks me up and down, taking in my baggy track-pants but I'm not intimidated - I'm actually heartened.

Great! I'm not the only beginner in their fifties taking their first class.

She replies with a French accent. 'I'm Marie, the fencing instructor but I only take on those who are willing to learn.'

My eager smile fades but I manage to reply. 'Wow, you're the instructor. Have you been fencing for long?' I speak quickly, hoping to cover my shock and creeping embarrassment.

'All my life. Fencing originated in Germany then it went to France, and then to Italy. It's still relatively unknown here. Why do you want to learn?'

'I've always wanted to,' I pause. I don't say that I grew up dreaming of being Robin Hood or one of the Three Musketeers or even the elusive El Zorro. I resist slashing an imaginary letter Z in the air and leaping about and instead I say. 'I like the art and the elegance of the sport.'

'You need great discipline, both physical and mental.'

The gym doors open and we stand aside as young footballers spill out. As we file inside Marie continues speaking to me. 'Run up and down and get warm. The others won't do it but you will feel the benefit of it.'

With that she strides off to the far end of the hall, her head held high and her nose in the air.

A chubby chap holds out his hand and smiles. 'I'm Bob. I teach the young ones - and the beginners - you're very welcome.'

'Great - thank you.'

A few adults have thrown their kit on the floor at the edge of the gym and are changing into their fencing gear but my enthusiasm is curtailed when I see the young boys around me. They all look very small and vulnerable.

I count seven children - all small - they barely reach my shoulder and I resit the urge to sing a chorus of 'Hi Ho, Hi Ho…'

No one is running up and down and I think that I'd look like a lunatic tearing up and down on my own, so I hover around Bob like a young puppy and he throws me a chest protector.

'Put that on!'

It's a - a breastplate. I think of Miranda Hart looking into the camera and mouthing the word: *breastplate.*

I want to giggle but I settle for a smile, bite my lips and

suppress a splutter of nervous laughter.

Beside me the dwarfs are slipping into their straight-jackets so I slide my arms inside surprised at the bulky heavy protection and feeling decidedly uncomfortable and upset - I'd always wanted a red cape. The zip is at the back and I can't reach it. I try and make eye contact with a twelve year-old hoping for a volunteer to 'do me up' but sensibly he averts his eyes. They all do. Thinking that it's maybe a female thing I walk down to the end of the hall and approach Marie.

She's now dressed regally and professionally in her white fencing suit. Much more elegant than my black baggy tracksuit and gaping straight-jacket.

I make a mental note to self: *Must buy fencing gear.*

Marie growls at me. 'You don't need to wear that now.' She turns to a tall, handsome swordsman called Oscar. Like her, he's dressed in white. His fencing outfit shows his narrow waist and broad shoulders. His serious brown eyes don't leave her face when she rattles off a few sentences in German then without taking a breath, she ends in English.'So, get her warmed up,' she says.

I turn away.

No Miranda: no camera and definitely no giggling.

He frowns seriously. 'We'll run eight widths of the hall,' he says. 'But it's busy tonight so we may have to dodge some people.'

I haven't run for over forty-five years, since my last sports day at junior school but now it seems I'm training with the elite fencing squad. I stand proudly to attention and I want to shout: '*All for one and One for All,*' but without a sword in my hand I'd look a right idiot. So, I follow him gallantly. Trotting behind, gazing at his gazelle-like legs and his broad shoulders, trying to look elegant. I suppress a splutter of laughter trying not to think of Miranda galloping her imaginary steed across the gym.

When we reach the far wall, he says, 'Let's pick up speed.'

Oh, let's!

He isn't joking. I run back across the gym chasing after this handsome twenty-year old like a cougar on heat. For the first time in over three decades I'm running and I'm also feeling very out of breath and extremely hot.

We're on our last lap and sprinting like we're going for an Olympic Gold when a boy steps mistakenly into my path. He screams. I gasp. He squeals and I duck. I dodge just time and avoid a nasty accident but I feel the angry heat of his gaze on my perspiring back as I trot bravely (and tiredly) back to Marie.

I'm panting hard. My breathing is heaving from my chest cavity in rasping sobs as if it's been imprisoned for eternity. I'm bent double hoping she hasn't witnessed the small incident: that's before I've even touched a sword - and I'm relieved when she ignores me and starts speaking to Oscar.

But it's another barked order and Oscar indicates for me to sit on the floor beside him. Lovely. But then we stretch - and stretch some more and I'm stretching muscles that have lain dormant longer than Mount Fuji. I'm ready to close my eyes. I'd be quite happy to lie back and rest but Oscar insists that we stretch just that tiny bit more. It's only when he gives me a small smile with his handsome hazel eyes that I'm encouraged and I just hope I haven't done any permanent damage.

I hurt. It hurts. My whole body is exhausted.

Oscar is Marie's best student and I stand up as as they take up their positions, trying to regain my breath wishing my face wasn't so hot wondering if I'll ever feel normal again.

The warm up is obviously over and I'm ignored so I wander back to Bob and the children at the other end of the hall. I'm hoping they won't recognise me as the Olympic athlete who crashed into them earlier.

'What do you want to do?' Bob asks me smiling.

Is there a bar? A gin and tonic would be nice.

'Would you like to join in here?' He nods at the group of small boys standing with him.

Hi Ho, Hi Ho.

'I'll give it a go,' I reply.

I smile when he hands me a sword. It's the first time I've ever held a real one so I weigh it professionally, tossing it from one hand to the other and weaving it in small ever decreasing circles feeling its weight. This is what it must have been like for Athos, Porthos, Aramis and d'Artagnan when they held their weapon.

Suddenly I want to leap and lunge like El Zoro. Maybe I could even get a black mask-

'Oops, that's the wrong one,' Chis says, taking it carefully from me. 'That's a Sabre, you need a Foil.'

'Oh, no. I thought my hair was fine.' I pat my head reluctant to give up my sword.

But he doesn't hear me or if he does, he doesn't smile.

With a Foil in my hand and my pulse racing excitedly I line up alongside the seven to fourteen-year olds. Conscious that I'm the tall, older one at the end of the row. But I stand with my shoulders back, upright and proud. We are all clad in straight-jackets and face guards.

We're like soldiers. White warriors.

All for One, I want to scream.

Wearing a face guard is like having a bird cage stuck on your head. It's like I'm underwater with a mask over my face and I'm listening to my own loud rasping breath. The warm up has exhausted me and I swat away the perspiration that trickles down my neck as if it's an annoying ant.

Bob takes us through the rudimentary steps; all new to me but familiar to the younger boys. He recaps on previous lessons reminding them of the necessary skills. Basically; bend your knees, balance and with your left arm in the air behind you, thrust forward with your right arm holding the sword - maintaining your balance equally and not bouncing. Professionally known as: On Guard, To Parry, The Riposte and To Lunge.

That is definite a Miranda word and one I wanted to repeat continuously:

Lungggge.

It's my nerves and fortunately I'm distracted.

I'm paired with James. He is the tallest boy and nearer my height than any of the others. He's also well padded so guess it won't hurt if I stab him.

Armed with my Foil and knowing how to step forward and then back again with my knees bent I'm excited. The tension is rising in me as quickly as my body temperature is heating my blood. All my childhood memories come racing back to me. Like when I was Robin Hood, pretending I was climbing trees in Sherwood Forest and brandishing my sword at the rich people saying I wanted to take their money and give it to the poor.

Poor James.

He takes my full onslaught.

My enthusiasm is mixed with my memories: Parry, Riposte and Lunge. I'm robbing Kings and Knights alike. I'm chasing men who want to kill the King. I'm in a battle and fighting warriors, protecting the castle, the tower, and the drawbridge.

Ten minutes of fielding my attack and James stands aside and removes his helmet. I imagine his face is the same shade of peach as mine and his cheeks are like giant throbbing beach-balls. He congratulates me and smiles gallantly. '5:4 – not bad for a beginner.'

'You were impressive,' I reply not realising he was keeping score. My ego is boosted and I puff out my chest. My childhood has been reawakened. I'm young again. I have a purpose. My cheeks glow and my chest heaves heavily.

As we catch our breath James tells me he's been fencing for a few years. He becomes my teacher and for a few minutes he gives me advice then he says. 'Don't waggle your Foil in small circles like I do, you're not at that stage yet.'

Um.

That doesn't sit well with me. I'm obviously not experienced enough for any *Foil waggling* and I can't pretend I don't feel a pang of disappointment but fortunately I'm distracted when I'm paired with a new boy.

He looks terrified.

Before we all begin again, fencing in pairs, Bob reminds us of the proper lunge positions and I put on my face guard. Once we start I quickly advance and the opposition beats a hasty retreat which only makes me more enthusiastic. I'm winning. I attack by tapping his sword away and quickly dipping my own point into his small chest and my *Foil* bends as I stab him. My energy, swordsmanship and manic eyes probably makes him step quickly backwards and he stumbles over his own feet.

I'm El Zoro. I take no prisoners. No matter how old they are.

I parry and I lunge.

Bob is clearly impressed. He stands between me and the boy.

'Good. Good. Well done. You've passed. Marie will take you on. You can go and join her.'

I want to punch the air with my fist. 'Fantastic.' But it doesn't seem appropriate so I strut – my best musketeer walk with my helmet tucked under my arm toward the elite group at the end of the gym where I firmly believe I belong.

I'm no longer a fifty-year old beginner - I'm one of the elite;

one of Marie's troops. She only takes the best.

She nods curtly at me.

We place our helmets on and she walks around me, staring at me like I'm an exotic specimen in a jam-jar.

'Let me look at you. Bend your knees, like this. Find your balance.'

I am at this moment still trying to find my breath. I'm panting heavily inside my face-mask and it's stifling. I'm like a heavy breathing psychopath. A mass murderer in one of those ghastly film that's on late and terrifies me. I'm even scaring myself.

I wonder if Marie can hear me?

'On guard,' she says raising her sword vertically to her

nose.

I do the same. I'm ready to fight. I will not be defeated. She would be tame compared to all the enemies I fought off growing up. I defeated all the baddies. I took their silver, their horses and I robbed their homes - and all to save the poor.

She may see the hungry look in my eyes or maybe she's aware of my shortness of breath because she lowers her defence and says crisply. 'This is a discipline of the mind and of the body. It takes practise. Not one hour a week but serious, dedicated time, hours of repetition. It's not how quickly you brandish your sword or how wild you are. It's how little you move it. That's where the skill lies. When you attack and throw your sword in wide movements then the power is lost.'

I'm reprimanded.

It dawns on me then that I have behaved like a middle aged, hysterical nutcase. I've been enthusiastically attacking my opponents. I'd expected a full-on swashbuckling adventure while all the young boys were cowering behind their face guards behaving professionally. I feel ridiculous. On top of that my calves ache and I'm exhausted but Marie's next programme consists of me standing and lunging at her torso.

She doesn't fight back.

'The point of your sword should hit me here.' She bangs her chest. 'Your Foil should bend like this.' She moves forward against my sword so it bends into an upward arch. 'Lunge again. Good. Very good!'

Once again, I'm encouraged and my youthful vigour and enthusiasm returns.

'Move forward with your front leg, slide in one

movement,' she orders. 'Not like this.' She imitates my three clumsy movements and I laugh and take off my helmet using the moment to cool down. I wish I'd brought some water with me. My face is pulsating like a giant plum and I'm giggling hysterically unwilling to meet her serious eyes.

She stares at me. She can't take her eyes off me. Then very slowly she says. 'I think that is enough for one day.'

I glance at the clock. There's still ten minutes of the class remaining but I have been dismissed.

We shake hands and I thank her.

'You will need your own equipment – if you come back.'

I nod. My breathing is failing me. Words fail me. My body has failed. I stand panting beside the wall. My helmet on the ground at my feet. It's hard to wiggle out of a straight jacket with the zip at the back so I give up. The rest of the class is fencing and I feign interest, watching the restrained lunge, riposte and parry.

It's all very civilised.

Not like in the films.

Why they have let me go early?Is my face too red?

Bob comes over to me. 'Are you going to have another go?'

'Marie seems to think I've had enough.'

'You'll get in the car on the way home and wished you'd had another go…' he smiles.

I nod. 'You're right.' I pick up my helmet and although my knees are still shaking and my muscles are aching there's nothing like a bit of excitement to give me a kick-start and a quiver of pleasure.

Bob partners me with Mark.

'This is a mega work out,' I say delaying the moment I would have to lunge, parry and repose. 'I never realised this fencing business took so much energy.'

'For me too.' He's mid-forties, ten years younger than me, and he tells me James is his son.

'He's a brave lad.' I can hardly speak. My head is dizzy and my throat dry. 'I think I was probably too eager with him.'

I put on my mask, raise my right arm and point my Foil at his chest. Pleased to be fighting a proper man.

On guard.

Mark is controlled, calm and sleek. All the things I'm not. But I do have enthusiasm on my side. It's *All for One.* I brandish my sword. I attack, parry and I lunge.

3:2.

I lose.

I pull of my helmet. Gasping. Thirsty and tired.

I like Mark and because he's an adult I think I can confide in him.

'I have to get into shape,' I gasp.

'It's great way to stay fit,' he agrees panting. His trimmed beard covers his red-hot cheeks.

Could I have beard envy?

I turn my back on him as if we're alone in a bedroom. 'Would you mind?'

He unzips me and I'm conscious that it's quite an intimate moment and he's extremely close to my sweating body.

'Wearing one of these is like being in the bake-off tent,' I laugh for distraction and he grins. 'Miranda Hart. Sue Perkins. Far too much television,' I continue babbling. My brain is whirling in another direction completely.

Maybe I should stick to baking?

NO never! Thank goodness I have a new past-time. A new hobby.

Fencing.

The class are changing into their normal clothes and Bob stands beside me. 'Did you enjoy it?'

He can't seem to take his eyes off my face and I beam back at him. Satisfied, excited and weirdly content. I don't tell him this is where my destiny lies and it's something I've always wanted to learn.

'Are you coming back next week?' he asks.

'Definitely.' My breathing is still heavy and my voice husky. 'And I'll bring some water with me next time.'

Thrilled to be part of the new elite group I wave and thank everyone in sight, beaming happily and as I leave the building my strut is confident. I imagine I'm dressed in high boots and a wide brimmed hat with feather plumes as I toss the long red cloak over my shoulder.

Outside in the fresh air my forehead is sweaty. My hair sticks out and my T-shirt is glued to my back. I ease myself gently into my car. My back is breaking and my muscles are aching like I've been chasing and galloping after bandits through a deep dark forest.

What an adventure.

I yawn.

Although it's February and only three degrees outside. I'm sweltering. I ease down the window and open the sunroof of my red Fiat 127. It slides back and I look up at the star studded night-sky just as Robin might have done in Sherwood Forest, or the Three Musketeers on one of their adventures. I'm pleased I'm not camping in any woodlands and I start the engine thinking of a cold shower and comfy pyjamas.

At the entrance to the sports centre my new group of friends are flowing out and onto the pavement. I raise my arm to James. He doesn't acknowledge me and he even appears to step back into the shadow of the building. Maybe a manic fifty-something-year-old now behind the wheel of a car, waving like an enthusiastic nutcase, scares him.

He doesn't appear to recognise me. I don't know why. I must have stabbed him at least twelve times.

'ALL FOR ONE,' I shout out of the sunroof but no-one shouts back.

They're probably terrified that I'll return next week.

End.

New Releases Mailing List

Sign up for the Janet's New Releases mailing list and get a free copy of the first book in the Culture Crime Series: MASTERPIECE. To download your free copy simply go to:

http://www.subscribepage.com/janetpywell

MASTERPIECE - The Blurb:

Mikky is planning the heist of her life.

But when opera diva Josephine Lavelle appears on the scene her plans start to unravel.

An investigative journalist is intent on uncovering Josephine's secret but Mikky faces a far greater threat from an unexpected source. She stands to lose everything, including her life…

How far will she go to pursue her dream?

A gripping crime thriller. An exciting, fast-paced novel involving an exciting heist, an unusual robbery, and an innovative thief. Her secrets will have you hooked in the first book of this debut trilogy.

Other books by Janet Pywell

Culture Crime Series:
Golden Icon (the prequel)
Masterpiece - Book 1
Book of Hours - Book 2
Final Script - Book 3 - due for publication spring 2018

Short Stories:
Red Shoes and Other Short Stories
Bedtime Reads - Bite-Sized Page Turners

Romance:
Ellie Bravo